Stars

Kayla Kimel

Thank you to everyone who has supported me throughout this tedious ordeal. Through the late night tears and excited plot breakthroughs. Thank you so much.

To Mack, for suffering through my endless questions and "BUT DOES THIS MAKE SENSE?". For helping me come up with a name, and giving me the hope to carry on.

To Kelsey, for forcing me to pick it back up after a yearlong break. For participating in NaNoWriMo with me, and being the best suffering partner a girl could ask for.

To Taylor, for giving me the harshest criticisms I've ever received, and for making me want to prove you completely wrong.

And to Tommy, for making me finish, dealing with my nervous breakdowns and helping me every step of the way.

I love you all.

I can't really tell you what exactly happened that day. The day where everything got supremely fucked up. But I can tell you what I imagined that happened, and my experiences coupled with the experiences of the people I've talked to since then should provide you with a pretty accurate picture. And who knows? Maybe one day when they clear out this godforsaken place and try to rebuild, maybe when they right the wrongs that they left to us to figure out, we'll know what actually happened. But in all honesty, I'm not writing this to tell you what happened that day and the days that followed. This is more like me putting my stamp on the world in the limited time that I may have left. What follows are my actual experiences as I remember them best, some are painful, some are happier but all are very real and true to me.

It was a normal Saturday in the late summer. There was some big shindig down in the centre of town, I hadn't been bothered to go or even find out all that much information about it. My parents were going, my dad because of the needed security for a crowd this large, my mom and younger sister just because. I was home, hanging around on the lawn enjoying the last days of warm weather and watching the new puppy romp around in the bushes. Like I said, it was normal. A scattered few neighbours had wandered around, going about their daily business before heading downtown. No one had stayed behind, I was alone on the otherwise quiet street and had decided to take advantage of that. The trees blew gently in the wind, the perfectly green and manicured lawns lending to the idyllic ambience of it all. Whatever shenanigans may have been going on downtown were blocked out by the music I was pumping through the open windows, but I sure as hell felt it when the earth moved the first time. I was thrown onto the grass and the dog ran, yelping, to my side. My world was upside down for a few minutes, and then the ground stopped shaking. What it left behind was a massive crack that ran lengthwise down the street, veering off to one edge and decimating a few houses. Stunned, I stayed where I had fallen, trying to make sense of it all.

I didn't know it then, but the square downtown had been since deserted aside from the stragglers who hadn't obeyed the commands that were being shouted from the loudspeakers. Now they were paying the price. Those who couldn't get away fast enough, the ones who had hung around hoping for some spectacle, were thrown through the air like a collection of rag dolls. The sky screamed and turned hot, expanding and demolishing everything that stood in its path in a cloud of destruction and pain. Buildings crumbled into dust, shrieking against the buckling ground that had been stable only minutes earlier. The concrete cracked, rippling from building to building until there was only a ring of devastation left behind. Bodies littered the ground, lifeless eyes staring up at the sky. Then where there had previously been a cacophony of noise, there now was silence.

At least, that's what I've been told. It was hard listening to the others recount their experiences. I had gotten off easy, even if I didn't know it then. And really, nothing made sense anymore.

Day 3

I spent two days in the house before I decided to do anything even remotely constructive. Two days spent migrating between the phone and the television, hoping for news or something. The former never rang, and the latter refused to even turn on. In the beginning I had just thought that maybe things had gotten shaken around in the earthquake, but after the fourth time of trying every appliance in my house I had to concede defeat. The phone lines were always busy and I took some hope from that. Maybe they were trying to call. Something had gone down at this event thing, and they had to stay there until the roads reopened. They couldn't get through because the lines were down, maybe a pole or two had been knocked over. These were the thoughts that got me through the first two days.

After my third morning of waking up on the couch and doing my now usual routine of checking the phone lines, electricity and street for any sign of my neighbours, I decided that enough was enough. For seventy-two hours I had been alone in this house by myself and I wasn't willing to wait around until I was found anymore. Besides, the smell coming from the refrigerator was enough to drive anyone out of the house.

"Mads, c'mon girl." I knew the dog was probably going to be more of a hindrance than a help but I couldn't just leave her behind. She was a puppy and if nothing else I was sure of, I knew I had to keep her around. After clipping her leash on I was at a loss. Where exactly was I supposed to go? The event grounds I guessed, even if I had no idea what kind of state it would be in, that was the best place to start. The last place I knew they had been.

The walk was quiet. I didn't encounter anyone on my way to the subway, and I was surprised that there was absolutely no traffic on the roads. The place was a ghost town, and I didn't see a single human being on the hour long walk. Cars were still neatly parked along the road leading to the event grounds and I had the eerie feeling that I had walked onto a movie set that was uninhabited by the actors that would make it seem real. Mads walked silently beside me, even the dog was upset by the creepy feeling of silence pressing in on us from all sides. Her ears were pinned flat against her skull, tail drooping and tight between her legs. For whatever reason that had suddenly possessed me to do so, I gave a shout. My voice echoed thinly along the road, bouncing back at me from the buildings that hadn't become broken crumbling hulks of their once former selves.

The further into the heart of the city we walked, the more I noticed the chaos that was popping up around me. When I had started walking only a few homes or buildings were cracked or broken, and definitely nothing serious. But now there were whole streets of two, three, seven houses in a row split down the middle, roofs caved in, windows smashed. More and more I suspected the possibility of an earthquake. That would explain the cavernous cracks that ran along the roads.

I slowed a bit when we were getting close, the torn flags fluttering weakly in what little wind there still was. Truth be told I was kind of afraid to advance into the square, afraid of what I would (or wouldn't for that matter) find. Mads strained at the leash and I let myself follow meekly behind her, though when I finally laid eyes upon the square I stopped in my tracks, snapping her backwards with my sudden loss of motion. My hand moved instinctively to cover my mouth, gaping wide in a shocked expression. In front of me was a body. And it wasn't only a singular feat. They were everywhere, splayed in awkward positions that the living would never have assumed. Blood dripped from them all, the bright red in stark contrast to their pale faces and bodies. The scent hit me like a brick wall, copper and salt and pennies.

"What... happened?" My voice, sharp against the stillness of the scene before me, sent some nearby birds squawking from their roosts. Crows I realized, waiting to set down upon the corpses when they were deemed ready for feasting on. Bile rose in my throat and I dashed to the nearest garbage can, emptying my stomach in a few heaves. I barely noticed the hands on my back, Mads' excited yipping, or the hair that was being pulled away from my face. When it was over, when I was finally able to straighten up and wash out my mouth with the water bottle from my bag I turned towards whoever was behind me, the first live person I had seen in days and nearly burst into tears.

"Zach." The word was a whisper that spluttered in my throat, my heart doing a half-hearted version of the skippity little jump that it used to do whenever he caught me by surprise. It probably didn't help that it was him I was meeting first, him of all people. A few sideways glances while chugging more water provided me with an overview of his physical appearance. He looked tired and dishevelled, I probably looked the same, but there were shadows under reddened eyes that weren't exactly caused by a lack of sleep. "Zach?" This time the name was a question. Though we were friends we weren't the closest. Yeah, we had had our nights staying up until four in the morning talking, but those hadn't been happening recently and I was mildly afraid to pry. But then again, and considering the present situation we now found ourselves in, it made sense. Didn't it?

"Alice." His hair had gotten longer, had it really been that long since I had seen him? "You haven't seen anyone either have you? Your parents never came home? I didn't see them... around." There was something in the way he said the last sentence that made me balk. Why the hesitation? I shook my head, hoping that he would continue. All he did was sigh and rub a hand across his eyes. "I mean, I didn't see them. You know." This time there was a gesture with his hand, and he waved it aimlessly behind him. Fearful, I peeked over his shoulder – was he always that tall? – and instantly dropped back down onto the balls of my feet, knees threatening to give way.

Rows upon rows of bodies circled the epicenter of what I assumed to be the detonation. The ripples of concrete seemed to be spreading from it, and bodies were snagged on the jagged edges of stone, thrown carelessly against benches and all of them had that same blank look. My mind searched for any point to grasp onto, for any reasoning that would keep me sane. Zach had said he hadn't seen them. Why had he been canvassing the bodies? I looked back at him; the blank look was mirrored in his eyes. "Zach?" His fists clenched at his side and he looked down at the ground, angry tears hidden behind the mass of dark hair. "Zachary… who was it?" I grabbed at one of his hands, unclenching his fist with my fingers. This was a new one, since when was I the one comforting him? It was always me having the breakdowns, needing to be coached back into reality with some gentle words and a hug or two.

"Zachary. C'mon Zach, let's sit down or something." Mads tugged at the leash that was looped tightly around my free hand, straining to sniff at his pants and begging for attention in whatever way she could. Though I nearly tripped both over the dog and the body I was trying so hard to ignore, I managed to lead us over to a secluded tree that had been stripped of its branches and had a hole gouged through the center, presumably from the shattered lamppost that was lying nearby.

There were several fairly uncomfortable seconds of silence in which I twiddled with the ripped hem of my pants and Zach stared down at his hands, I had untangled mine from him when we sat down. "If you don't want to tell me it's totally-"

"It was my dad." He cut me off, flinching at saying the words themselves. He still had the tone of someone who didn't fully believe in the reality that he was being confronted with. I didn't know what exactly to do, he had dropped my hand willingly enough, and what exactly did you do to comfort someone under these circumstances? "Zach, I'm so-" Again he cut me off with a wave of his hand. Was I not supposed to say that? I didn't know what to do; nobody had ever prepped me for this. "Zach." Why was it that all I could manage was his name? I rested a hand on one of his shoulder, a little taken aback when he instead wrapped his arms around me, shaking slightly. It took a while to realize that he was actually trying to hold in the silent sobs, so I squeezed him back.

We sat like that for however long. I didn't dare move until I knew he had composed himself. When he finally let me go he turned away, probably embarrassed that he had broken down like that in front of me. But for all anyone knew we only had each other right now. The thought struck me as romantic, not exactly the best time for it. "What happened? All I remember is being on the lawn and the sounds and the earth was moving." I gave him the abridged version, telling him about the no electricity and the phones being dead and not hearing anything for three dreadful days. I tried not to emphasize that part. After all, it wasn't me who had recovered a body of my dad. Speaking of, where the hell were they? Dad, mom and Katie had all been here. How had they escaped the blast? The sinking realization of my family's disappearance began to set in and I could feel a chill creeping through my bones.

"I don't know, I honestly wasn't here for that much longer than you. I was at home sick when it happened, just barely managed to get out of bed before the roof caved in over the bedrooms. Then when I could stand without passing out I came down here. I heard you shout." He had managed to deal with things pretty fast, though he was kind of sketchy on the details on when exactly he had found the body. And what exactly did he want to do with that? It wasn't a question I was raring to ask.

"We should do something. I'm starving; I don't know how easy it'll be for you to hold down some food at the moment, but what if we eat and regroup and figure out a plan. There are still so many people unaccounted for." I let the last sentence hang in the air for a moment too long, and I started to doubt any positivity I may have displayed. What did I think I was going to find? If there hadn't been any people for three days, what were the chances that we were going to find some joint with a cook and a waitress to take our orders? Hell, a grocery store would do at this point. "If that's cool with you." I felt like I was treading on eggshells, but he looked composed enough after the breakdown.

"What? Oh yeah, food. Good idea." Alright, not quite the enthusiasm that I was looking for at the moment but it was better than nothing. I took a moment to chide myself for not taking things slower, the man had just lost his father and if it was I in his shoes I knew I would be a wreck right about now. God only knew, I might just be in his shoes later on, though he had said he hadn't found anyone from my family, and it was probably better to prepare myself as best as I could right now. "Yeah." Apparently he had made his decision and stood in one fluid motion, holding out a hand to help me up.

We walked in silence for the most part. He walked slightly behind me, eyes downcast and hair covering his face, and I had my eyes peeled for any signs of other people or (I was holding my hope out on this one) my family. I didn't see anyone on the walk, and Mads did her part by sniffing out any lead which, every time, brought my hope up and then crashing down when every scent proved negative for living humans. Small talk didn't seem like much of an option at the moment and I wasn't going to press Zach any further then he was willing to go. Nor did I want to make him uncomfortable about prying. But I was curious. Before we made a plan, would he want to go back and bury his father? Was it even possible for two people? I made a mental note to keep an eye out for shovels or any kind of wreath or statue to put at the head of a grave, at the very least I had a marker in my bag, leftover from some school project that had just resulted in a marker being tossed haphazardly into the depths of my backpack. School, that seemed so far away and unimportant now, and to think I had previously been so excited about my acceptance into a stellar art program and a pretty decent university. That was due to start in a week or two, but it was now the furthest thing from my mind. And in all honesty, what were the chances that things would get all sorted out in fourteen days? Slim to none.

The store, my last real hope for finding someone, was just as empty as the ghost-town streets had been. The smell coming from the meat section was comparable to that which had been leaking out of my fridge, just on a much larger scale and I cringed from outside as I looped Mads' leash around a locked shopping cart. Instead we steered towards the produce, grabbing some of the sturdier looking fruit and a box of granola bars. At the very least, with these we wouldn't have to worry about rotting food. The cash register stumped us. "Do we leave money or like…?" My voice trailed off, staring down at the closed off register. It seemed ridiculous to leave money for unattended, old food but my upbringing and societal norms told me that I should leave the change anyways. "I dunno, I don't have any cash on me. Plastic only, which doesn't have much of a use with no electricity."

"Point taken." I scrounged around in my pockets for money, coming up with a crumpled five that I tucked underneath the closed drawer so that the weathered edge was visible. "Not exactly enough but it's the smallest bill I have. And never know, might need the twenty for something later on." Or later on we just might not pay for what we took, would that make us looters? Probably, and I didn't exactly like the thought.

Taking our contraband back outside and untangling Mads from the ball of leash and knots that she had become in our absence, we were at a loss again. It seemed like a good idea to just stay put for a minute, maybe in the hopes that someone else would wander across our path but as the hours whittled away from late morning to early afternoon we had to concede defeat and I decided to broach the subject that had been bothering me earlier in the day. "Zach, your dad.

We can go back and give him a proper burial or something. I can help if you want. There's a hardware store around here, and the park is right next door. It's probably not the best thing to do in this situation but it'd provide you with some closure I think. But it's entirely your call. Don't let me talk you into anything you're not comfortable with." I barely breathed throughout my statement, worried that if I paused he would contradict me or break down again. But he didn't, he stayed silent through the entire thing and looked at me with surprise. Like he hadn't even considered the option of burying his father.

"Yeah, I think that's a pretty good idea. I mean, I don't want to just leave him there." Was he thinking of the crows that I had scared away when I called out? I sure as hell was. The silence deepened to an almost uncomfortable state before he spoke again. "Yeah. Help me look for something to mark a grave with?" He was taking it well. I had blanched at the idea of burying my hamster a few years ago, and when it came down to it I had just stood in the backyard with my spade crying until my mom took pity on me and sent me away until Marbles was buried. So the fact that he was able to so stoically face the idea of burying his own flesh and blood was admirable.

"Sure." I nodded my assent, not really trusting myself to not say something stupid at this point. Both of us busied ourselves with the task at hand, separating to canvas store windows until I shouted out a floral place and we went in, noting the stones that carried sentimental messages. I picked out a wreath I thought was suitable and Zach rummaged around amongst the stones until he was satisfied. I didn't rush him. How could I? This time we didn't leave money.

Taking a wide arc around the bodies, we moved towards the park, shouldering the shovels that we had picked up off of the sidewalk sale nearby. I let Zach take the lead, and he paced amongst the bushes and benches for quite a while before he found the final resting place for his father. I was several feet away, leaning against the handle of the shovel, the blade shoved firmly into the ground. With him busy and no danger of our eyes meeting I took the rare opportunity of really looking at him, something that I hadn't allowed myself to do for an extremely long time. Aside from looking sadder he was the same guy I had known for a little over a year, the same guy who had offered me the basement couch and a ride there and back if I ever needed a place to crash. He still had the same dark hair, a little bit too long and a lot unruly, and even darker eyes. The same warm feeling fluttered into the pit of my stomach as when he had actually offered, and I could vaguely remember choking back tears at the time. It was still him, no matter the loss.

He looked up suddenly, apparently finished with marking off the gravesite. "Alice." If I hadn't been paying attention I might have missed him calling me. I unearthed the blade of my shovel and strode over, keeping an eye on Mads who was happily sniffing around some trees. "I've uh, marked it off, not too big because I want to get it done tonight." This was harder for him then he was letting on, it was easier for him to hide it when we were in constant motion, keeping ourselves busy and his mind occupied. I understood how he did it when we broke the ground, keeping a steady digging pace. The monotonous motion dulled my brain, hopefully providing some relief for him as well. Hours slipped by as we dug, and by the time the hole was deemed respectable enough for the body, I was sore and stiff, my legs and face streaked with dirt. The break we took was quiet, and we lingered over our water bottles to avoid facing what came next.

We'd have to move the body, funny how it had changed from being his father to just another nameless corpse in a few short hours, from the stone grounds into the park. I hadn't meant to think of him like that. But there were just so many bodies around, and the blood was so thick. Though it wasn't that far of a walk, we would be laden down with a body, which was actually pretty creepy. I had never been one to be happy and interested in the grosser aspects of life on earth and death was something I had never really experienced before today. The idea of carrying a body, carrying it with dignity and lowering it into a hole in roughly the same manner, was kind of daunting. Truth be told I didn't quite know how that was going to work out, but it was something I wasn't going to be squeamish about, not when it was something so important to Zach.

Not that I wanted to push him into going faster or anything, but the sky was already beginning to darken and we still had to figure out a plan for the night. Would we split up and go back to our respective homes? As much sense as that made it wasn't exactly the option that I was rooting for. It wasn't because it was him. No matter who I had managed to attach myself to I wouldn't want to split up at this point in time, not without knowing what we were up against. Not that we were up against anything per say, but we didn't know anything at all. "Are you ready Zach?" I was as ready as I would ever be, and was grateful when he nodded. The sooner we could get this over with the better.

The walk over was painful. I matched his pace, but I could tell that he was mildly uncomfortable with me being here, as happy as he had been previously. I understood that this was a private affair and would retreat as soon as I possibly could, but I had to help him carry his father back to our home-dug grave. This time the silence seemed more respectful and sombre then awkward and uncomfortable. We carried the body through the street. I stumbled a bit on the curb but managed to stay upright. I tried to focus on anything else but the gruesome task we had at hand. And all I could feel was his father's cold, clammy skin against my palms. I focused on watching my step; picking my way carefully through the ruin laden streets.

Zach, carrying what was left of his father under the arms walked backwards towards our grave, lowering himself in first so that we could arrange the body in a dignified way. He folded his father's hands across his chest and rummaged around in his pockets, extracting a wallet. Before I could ask what he was doing, he took a family photo out of it and placed it on top of his father's clasped hands. I took this as my cue and backed off, leaving the two of them in the grave. Mads trotted over, laying her head on my thigh after I had arranged myself on the ground. She sighed quietly, eyes rolling over towards where Zach was completely obscured by our mound of dirt. We stayed there until he lifted himself out of the grave, not daring to move as he sat on the edge, staring down at what he was giving up.

After a while I moved to stand behind him, Mads peering over the edge with that characteristic puppy interest. Zach didn't speak, simply placing his hand over the one that I had rested on his shoulder, my message of comfort received as best as he could. We stayed like that until the sun began to set, then moved to place the dirt as gently as we could back into the hole. His eyes were red again and I pretended not to notice, focusing completely on the task at hand. When we were done he threw the shovel to the ground, walking away a few meters before coming to a rest away from me. I looked to Mads, making sure she stayed away from the mound, before fetching my wreath and placing it at the top of the grave, making sure to leave room for Zach's headstone before backing off once more. This time I didn't sit and watch, but instead curled into a ball on the lawn, rubbing blades of grass between my fingers while I waited.

Time passed slowly, and I think I fell asleep while Zach said his goodbyes. The next time I opened my eyes, the sky was a deep red and I could see him sitting cross legged by my head. When he saw that I was awake he stretched, all signs of grief momentarily erased from his face while a grim determination took its place. "We need to figure out our next plan of action."

"Can we stay together?" The words were out before I even fully realized what exactly was coming out of my mouth and the childishness of my plea. "I mean. I don't want to stay alone again." Whatever, might as well try to explain myself as best as possibly so he would at least know why I was being a fool.

"No, I understand." He rubbed the back of his neck absently and I knew I wasn't the only one who wasn't exactly comfortable with being alone again. Who knew if we would be able to find each other if we split up for so long. "What I meant was where. I don't know about your place, but mine was destroyed."

"Mine's liveable I guess, but it's kind of far and my street was essentially split into a crapload of pieces. I really don't want to climb across those chasms."

"Fair enough. I don't know, there's a hotel near here. If we stay on the ground floor, I don't want to have to run down seventeen flights of stairs in case anything happens, there's probably an empty room or two. And they might even have a back up generator, plus a kitchen. It works well enough." I agreed with this on the stipulation that we scammed a bag of dog food for Mads, so before we set off for the hotel Zach swung a hefty bag of food over one shoulder and I grabbed a few cans just in case. The hotel wasn't far, and though the sliding doors confused us for a few minutes, we did find a side entrance that lead us into the lobby. Then we hit yet another snag.

"Key cards." I swore under my breath, spotting the dangly little plastic cards that were located behind the desk. "Now what? The doors are electronic."

Zach thought for a moment, rummaging behind the abandoned desk and in whatever drawer he could find until he came up with a hefty ring of keys, tossing them to me before shouldering the bag again. "Let's just hope they have some kind of other way to open them up, or maybe we can find the manager's suite or something like that. Stairs or no stairs, this is probably the best place we can sleep tonight." He thought for a moment, regarding the basement door that was labeled as employees only. "Or maybe we should try to hit up a generator first. Find a switchboard or something downstairs." More rooting around in the drawers, this time by me, yielded a flashlight that turned on after smashing it enough times off of the top of the desk.

We stood at the top of the dark basement stairs, a creepy feeling crawling over my skin as the wave of cold air rushed up to meet us. Sensing my hesitation, Zach loosened the flashlight from my grip, put down the dog food bag and grabbed my hand, leading me down the stairs. I didn't normally like basements even if they were brightly lit and this was anything but. The wavering light of the flashlight beam only illuminated a small patch of the stairs in front of us, and the temperature dropped drastically. When we hit the landing Zach let go of my hand, swinging the flashlight into a wide arc and resting it on the miracle that was the back up generator. "This is good." He moved towards it, lifting up a panel and flipping a few switches, locating the electrical panel and checking that as well. Within moments the generator began to produce a steady hum, warming up I assumed and after a little longer of a wait the lights flickered on and off, plunging us back into darkness before switching back on.

"Yes!" I jumped up and down in the air, grinning like a fool and envisioning a hot shower to scrub at the caked on dirt. Clothes would be a bit of a problem, but we could do laundry and I was sure there were pyjamas in the gift shop on the main floor. This could work. "Shall we?" Suddenly there was more of a bounce in my step, and a slighter one in his as well, and so we returned to where we had left Mads and wandered into an adjoined room.

"Ladies first?" He gestured towards the bathroom with a mock bow and I grinned again despite myself. This was more of the guy I had known previous to all of this shit.

"Nah, I'm going to wander down to the gift shop. Pick up some pjs and a toothbrush, I know I'm going to kill for one of those in the morning." I ignored his intonation of 'your loss' and waited until the door clicked shut behind him and I heard the steady downpour of the showerhead. "Mads, stay." I commanded the puppy, making sure she would listen before I backed out, walking cheerfully down the hall and exploring as I went. A chlorinated smell as I got closer to the lobby confirmed that there was a pool here, the confirmation bringing me back to the reality of the normal life I had lived before things had started to go down. The gift shop wasn't far from there, and I wasted no time in piling pyjamas for both of us, along with assorted toiletries and some snacks into a bag. I was looking over some paperbacks that were by the cash register when I heard a soft footstep behind me and hands wove their way around my waist before I could even move. "Zach, nice try." I tried to move the hands but they refused to budge and it was then that I turned around, shocked at the unfamiliar man who stood before me, hands moving back up until one rested in the messy ponytail that I had secured my hair into while we were grave digging. His hand clenched and he gave a sharp tug that brought tears to my stinging eyes and I gasped involuntarily.

The man had the weathered look about him that I usually associated with farmers or people who had seen a lot, large tanned arms covered in tattoos, chapped hands. But his face wasn't smiling; instead it was twisted into a grimace that sent chills into the backs of my knees, which buckled slightly. The hand holding my hair kept me from hitting the ground, or even twisting in a way that would allow escape. "What do you want? Who the hell are you?"

He chuckled darkly, moving towards me until my back was pressing into the edge of the counter in the hopes of lessening the space between us. Panic choked my throat, especially when he fumbled with the waistband of my jeans, running a thumb between the inside seam and now exposed strip of flesh. "What if I show you what I want, instead of telling you? Wouldn't want to ruin the surprise." His voice dripped honey and ice, grating against the edge of my brain. When I tried to dart to the side he grabbed a firmer hold of my hair and wasted no time in punching me hard in the stomach, making me double over in pain and a lack of oxygen causing sparks to fly in front of my eyes. I tried to gasp out a scream but he hit me hard on the back of the neck, finally letting go of my hair simply because I had dropped to the ground, darkness obscuring my vision for a few seconds.

Again the overwhelming urge to throw up rose in the back of my mind, and I could taste the acidity in my mouth but I was still too stunned to manage a sound, let alone the motion of vomiting. I could hear the clinking sound of a belt being undone, followed by my hands being drawn behind my back and the belt wrapping around them, the plastic cutting painfully into my wrists. It was then, confronted with the startling reality that what was about to happen was something that I could not allow to happen, that I managed a scream. It was also then that I realized Zach was in the shower, and the sound of the water and plumbing would most likely cover up any sounds of a scuffle. For all I knew he sang in the shower. And I had left Mads behind, my last line of defense in a situation like this.

With the realization that there was no help coming that gave me another burst of energy and I thrashed for all I was worth, allowing me to flip over so that I was no longer on my stomach and was facing my attacker who had a significant amount of weight on my ribs. I had managed to elbow him in the face, one eye was rapidly swelling and he backhanded me for my efforts, a slap that sent my head spinning once more. Blood welled in my mouth and I spat it at him, my last act of defiance. I was tired, bruised and my energy was being shattered, I was already exhausted from shovelling and burying Zach's father, not to mention emotionally sapped.

I screamed again, a half-hearted thing that was more of an attempt not to pass out more than anything when I suddenly felt the weight being lifted off of me. I rolled onto my side, coughing and spluttering, grateful for the sudden lack of weight. When my vision stopped swimming I looked over to where the sounds were now coming from, relieved to see both Mads and Zach tearing into my assailant. Zach was only in his jeans, water dripping from his soaked hair as he pinned the larger man to the ground, using his better position and the fact that Mads had a hold of one of the mans ankles to keep him down. A constant stream of swear words were pouring from his swollen lips, and the eye that I had hit was now swelling to the point where the eye itself was only a faint slit.

I struggled to my feet, ripping the loosened belt from my wrists and rubbed the feeling back into my hands, my eyes jumped crazily from one surface to the next until I had found something that suited my needs. One of those old school giant glass iced tea bottles, the neck felt cool in my palm as I swung it up and across, the bottle connecting with the mans skull with a thickening thud that sent vibrations running up my arm. Man and bottle dropped to the carpet as I panted, Mads let go of her death grip on his ankle, blood dripping from her tiny teeth, and wandered over to me, nudging her face into my leg. My face still stung from the slap and my ribs felt bruised but other than the sense of shock that was creeping through my bones I was alright.

As I stood shaking, Zachary got to work attaching some thick twine that he had found to the man's arms, binding his wrists like mine had been before. The shaking got worse and my knees buckled, I hit the ground with a wince but at least I was more stable now. The blood, metallic and salty in my mouth was still a mild pain in the ass and there was nothing more that I wanted than to take a shower right now. Some hot water and powerful scrubbing might make me feel clean again, but this time the dirty feeling wasn't just due to the mud and caked on dirt that was streaked across my skin. Zach finished whatever he had been doing, I had lost track once I hit the ground, and came over to me, kneeling down and gently pushing Mads out of the way when she tried to jump up and lick his face.

"Are you alright? Did he do anything before I got here?" His words brought back the feeling of fingers along my waist, burning the skin along the band of my jeans. But that wasn't what he was asking, so I shook my head no, tears filling my eyes. Damn it, I hadn't wanted to cry. Not right now anyways. In the shower, yeah I was okay with that. But definitely not in front of him.

"Yeah, fine." Well, that was as much as he was going to get out of me without me actually bursting into tears. And boys generally weren't all that good with tears. "Shower. Please." Awesome, a grand total of four words, a new high score. I got to my feet, probably trying to prove that I was more okay than I sounded, and shuffled in the general direction of the door, Mads following at my heels and nearly tripping me up once or twice in her concern. Damn dog, now was not the time to not let me out of her sight. Zach stayed behind me, close enough to touch, his presence at my back reassuring after the ordeal. The pair of them followed me back to the adjoining rooms.

"Here's the deal. We're going to lock and blockade your door. And I'm going to stay in mine in case you have any problems." It was probably more for his sake than for mine but I nodded anyways, not wanting him to beat himself up for not getting to me sooner. As it stood I wasn't thinking clearly, but now that I was presented with the plan I could acknowledge that it was a good idea. And probably something that we should consider doing that night, though I doubted I would be getting very much sleep.

He helped me move the dresser to stand in front of the door, both of us grunting against the heavy piece of furniture as it snagged on the carpet. Once that part was over I fed Mads, and heard the soft click of the door as he retreated to his room. There I stood, in the middle of the carpeted floor, counting to ten in my head like my dad had taught me and breathing slowly to try and calm myself down. Once sure that I wasn't going to pass out under the steady stream of water I undressed and hopped into the bathroom, closing the door firmly behind me. Mads began throwing herself against the door almost immediately so I left it ajar.

This apparently satisfied her, she lay in the doorway, face pointed towards the shower while I got in. The hot water was scalding; I had turned it up as far as it would go to make the impending shivers retreat and bring some warmth back to my icy skin. I was in there for a lot longer than my usual showers, partially because I had a bit of a meltdown where no one could hear me and also because the dirt was still running down my legs in large clumps before I would consider myself actually clean. When both my body and mind felt sufficiently clean I turned the water off and stepped out, wrapping one of those warm fluffy hotel towels around myself and stepping over Mads who was just struggling to wake up. Apparently the steam had made her lull off.

"C'mon girl," I nudged her with my foot, clutching the towel. The pyjamas and other toiletries I had picked up were still lying on my bed from when I had dropped them carelessly upon re-entering the room. Hopping into the pants, toothbrush tucked into the back pocket, I hastily pulled on the shirt while I knocked on the door that separated our two rooms. I could vaguely hear Zach pacing and muttering to himself, so I put on a brave face to show that I was completely over the situation and hopefully make him feel better about everything. Hopefully it was convincing enough, and I had only seconds to wipe the thoughtful expression off of my face and replace it with a small smile before he opened the door that separated us.

"Hey. Just wanted to let you know that I didn't drown or anything and here," I held out the pyjamas and toothbrush that I had picked up for him. "I grabbed these from the gift store before you showed up. But I totally guessed on your size. They're a drawstring pair though, so it shouldn't be that big of a deal right?" Alright fine, I was babbling, one of my signs of nervousness but it wasn't like he knew that. We hadn't spent that much time together for him to be picking up those subtle hints that my mom had always been so fantastic at spotting.

"Uh, yeah. Thanks." He peered into my face, maybe he could tell that I was covering up, and took my offerings gently. We both stood awkwardly in the door for a while, neither of us sure of what to say. "I guess I should like, get changed." I nodded dumbly, backing out of the doorframe so he could close it between us again and moving to the bed, unsure of what else to do.

Mads scrambled up to join me, laying her head on my stomach and looking up at me. I knew she wouldn't be letting me out of her sight for a while so I sighed, scratching the top of her head. "Overprotective little puppy dog."

"Yeah, I noticed that as well." I looked up in surprise at the sound of his voice; Zach stood in the door, leaning against the frame, arms crossed across his chest. He had gotten dressed and I had guessed pretty accurately, just another one of my extremely useless skills. "I was wondering if you were hungry, wouldn't blame you if you weren't, but we should probably get some sugar or something into both of us before we collapse. It was a hard day today." He was right of course, though it wasn't as bad as it had been before, I was still trembling, especially my hands. "I figured we could hit up the kitchen, it's gotta be somewhere around here. Or we could go scavenging. There's another grocery store near here, and judging by the state of our clothes, that might be another stop to hit up."

"Makes sense." I wasn't hungry but knew I should be, burying my shaky hands in Mads' fur. And it did make sense. As much as I abhorred the idea of more petty thefts, I knew our clothes wouldn't be all that comfortable when the mud and muck dried. We could always utilize the sinks and such to wash them clean, but the chances of that denim being clean and dry before morning wasn't likely. Morning, now there was a dizzying thought. What the hell were we going to do tomorrow? What was our plan? I liked to live my life in an organized fashion, not with a step-by-step plan or anything foolish like that, but routine was comforting, as was knowing what to expect next. I pushed the frightening thoughts out of my mind before they spiralled somewhere darker.

We decided to leave the dresser where it stood, thus making my room virtually inaccessible unless you went in through Zach's first. I clicked Mads' leash back on her collar, she strained away from me in her excitement, and quietly left my room, closing the adjoining door behind us. Zach's was as neat as mine had been. Neither of us had thought to bring anything with us when we had left our respective houses. We'd either have to make a trip back or pick up some new supplies. God knew when anything would begin to make sense again and it was best to be prepared for anything. I broached the subject with Zach as he turned off the generator, better to save the power for when we really needed it and neither of us really wanted to draw any more undesirables to our little hideaway.

"What do you think happened exactly? We both heard the explosions, saw the remnants of the earthquakes but there weren't nearly enough... bodies to account for a packed event. And I know there were tons of people there, my entire neighbourhood was emptied out." The basement, just a little spookier now that we knew there were other people around, was quiet enough as we tromped back up the stairs, the flashlight's feeble beam providing us with a tiny stream of light. Batteries, those would have to be picked up as well, and I added them to my mental list.

"I have no clue. They have to have been moved somewhere. Maybe they're all still alive. Nothing else makes sense right now, especially not that." He stopped, throwing an arm out to stop me. I looked out of the hotel doors, squinting my eyes to stare through the glass.

"Is that... Is that a giraffe?" Maybe I was more traumatized than I thought I was, because there was absolutely no way that this animal could be picking its careful way through the shattered concrete, backlit by the setting sun. "I must have hit my head. That's not possible." But even Mads was regarding it with a quiet curiosity, ears cocked and head tilted as she took in the sight of the giant figure of the giraffe.

"Well unless we're both hallucinating about the same thing, which is possible though pretty unlikely, there is a giraffe walking down the street. What the hell?" Our faces were pressed almost against the glass, eyes tracing the giraffe's slow progress as it made its way down the street. "What the hell is even going on? Nothing makes sense anymore."

This was definitely a new mystery to ponder, but neither of us gave it as much thought as we should have. Instead we continued on our merry way, taking a wide detour around the animal as we headed into the nearest clothing store. There we separated, though I noticed how Zach looked up at me every once in a while as I perused the aisles, trying to grab stuff that wasn't exactly the same calibre of what I normally wore. Even though we had stores at our disposal there was no telling where we would end up or where this series of extremely confusing events would lead us. It made the two of us more cautious than usual, and I shot worried glances at him when I could tell he wasn't looking. Just seeing him reassured me a little every time, and I counted my blessings that I wasn't completely alone in this crazy situation that we had ended up in.

The dressing rooms were a bit of a pain in the ass, as neither of us wanted to be caught completely unawares if anyone else came into the store, and Zach had a bit of a problem with me standing guard, especially if he was going to be, literally, caught with his pants down. Eventually we agreed that the best compromise was for me to stand behind the clothing rack, unspotted by anyone who might come through the doors but close enough to him to whisper through the door.

"Overprotective puppy dog." I muttered under my breath as he went first, disappearing behind the mirrored door. Though I had to admit that him caring was sweet, it was destined to be a bit of a bother, especially if he insisted on my protection no matter what. Apparently chivalry wasn't dead, the opposite of what I had been lead to believe by a few of my female friends. The thought brought a pang to my stomach and I choked up for a minute or two. Would I see them again? Would I see my parents, the rest of my family, my class mates, anyone ever again? The thought was sobering, and I was caught up in the onslaught of memories that came with it until he tapped on my shoulder, apparently happy with his choices.

"Your turn." He took the leash from me, patting Mads to calm her down and took up my vacated spot behind the clothing rack. I grabbed my pile of clothes, unlocking the door from the top and separated myself from the pair of them with the click of the door. I had guessed pretty accurately once again, my sizes hadn't changed much from the last time I had gone shopping and it didn't take me long to settle on a few choice items that were fairly durable and easy to pack.

"Socks, we're probably going to need more socks." I advised quietly, knowing that any sounds could give our position away if anyone came in. But seeing how I hadn't heard the tinkling of the bell over the door, I assumed that we were safe enough for now.

He made a noncommittal noise in the back of his throat to let me know that he had heard me and I returned from the dressing room, taking the leash back from him and pushing Mads back to the ground. "Down girl."

"I was thinking. Do you think that the zoo exhibits might have collapsed in the earthquake? If it was powerful enough to split the streets and destroy a few buildings, I'm sure it could have taken down a chain link fence or two." His guess seemed plausible enough, and it would explain the legendary sight we had both agreed on hadn't been imaginary.

"Makes enough sense." I bagged our items, reaching behind the counter to grab a few extras just in case. "We should probably keep on our toes even more then, there were more dangerous animals in that zoo if I do recall." Like carnivorous cats, giant wolves and even a bear or two. Not exactly a crew that I would enjoy meeting in a dark alleyway late at night. "Maybe we should get some bats or something? A crowbar or two would probably help us feel a bit more secure." It was something else to consider, what exactly were we up against here? A few animals, those could be dealt with. Hopefully. But did our problems extend past a few salivating jaws studded with fangs? That was definitely a question that needed answering, and soon.

A few more stops before we returned home, we stocked up on fruits and veggies, as many as we could carry that wouldn't spoil quickly, batteries and just some odds and ends, mostly medical things to have just in case. The twilight that had greeted us when we first left the hotel had now retreated into full blown night time, the darkness shushing the city and making everything seem just a little more sinister. Once I had jumped at the third garbage can in a row, seeing scary faces everywhere I looked, Zach took my hand and we both returned to the hotel. Both doors now blocked off, we ate our meal in an amiable silence, the two of us becoming more comfortable with each other as the time wore on. Mads fell asleep at the foot of Zach's bed and I knew that I should be getting some sleep as well. I stretched, unlocking the kinks that had formed from me sitting on the floor and regarded him, stretched out on the floor and staring off into space. No part of me wanted to leave, I would be more than happy passing out on his floor, but I figured he would want some space after everything we had gone through together and apart.

"I'm going to head off to bed." I murmured, not quite wanting to bring his attention back to me, and stood. "C'mon Mads." The puppy opened one eye to stare at me for a moment before getting to her feet, disgruntled with the fact that I had woken her up. "I'm not exactly a heavy sleeper, especially under the current circumstances, so if you yell I'll wake up." Enough procrastinating, it was time to leave him alone so I backed towards the door, freezing with my hand on the knob when I heard him return my goodbye.

"Sweet dreams." Funny how one little phrase, one that I had heard uttered thousands of times by my parents, could weaken my knees in the smallest of ways. Even at a time like this. It was mildly surprising, but I tried to act like it hadn't affected me at all. That was the one thing I was good at. So far he hopefully hadn't had a clue of my feelings for him in the past, and if he had he had been kind enough not to bring them up. Granted, it wasn't exactly a time for reminiscing and light talk when we could be planning our next moves, but he would have brought it up if he knew, right? The thoughts pushed me through the door and into bed, the curtains closed against the starry night. I had never seen as many stars in the city before and I opened the heavy cloth so I could get a good look at the sky, hoping that they would calm my mind and help me sleep. There was no hum from the generator, we had agreed that keeping it off would be the best bet to conserve energy and had let ourselves in with the keys we had found, and the city itself was silent. It was hard to fall asleep, my thoughts bounced around in my head and I wasn't used to the complete silence that had blanketed my once rowdy metropolis.

The hours slipped by slowly and I had to suppress the urge to get up and knock on the door. Either the silence next door meant that he was awake as well, staring at the ceiling like me or that he was just a quiet sleeper. Mads snored quietly at my feet and I matched my own breathing to hers, eventually slipping into a series of nightmares that ultimately woke me up. I was screaming into my pillow and sat up with a jerk, hugging my knees to my chest and panting as if I had just run a marathon. It took a moment for everything to register, and when I spotted the figure sitting at the end of my bed I jumped a bit, scuttling away before I fully woke up, the edges of my nightmare disappearing and my brain finally realizing that there was no danger. Zach was staring at me with some concern, perched on the end of my bed and before I could question him he spoke.

"I heard you screaming and ran in here. You've kept this up for a while but I couldn't get you to wake up."

"Sorry." I replied meekly, rubbing my eyes in an attempt to push the images out of my mind. "I just... I just can't get it out of my mind." My voice hitched in an embarrassing way and I quickly wiped the tears from my eyes. Damn, this was happening again? What the hell, there was no shower to escape to this time and before I knew it I had burst into full-blown tears. Loud enough for him to notice, because next thing I knew he had scooted to sit beside me, wrapping an arm around my shoulder and pulling me into his chest. We sat like that for a while before the crying subsided and I felt drained enough that my eyes began to droop. Before I could even utter a thank you or anything of the like, my brain disconnected and I dropped off to sleep.

Day 4

The sunlight streaming in through the window woke me up eventually. I had never really woken up early in the past but now was apparently an exception to my inner clock. I was confused for a moment, why the hell was Zach in my bed? Then I remembered the night before, how I had had nightmares and screamed, sending both of us into a panic. I could also remember the crying jag that had happened against my will and stifled a groan, not exactly wanting to wake up my bedmate. Somehow I managed to slip out of bed without making him stir, a feat I could only call impressive, and shuffled off to the bathroom, desperately wanting to wash my teeth. By the time I was showered, dressed and had munched a granola bar or two he still wasn't up so I stretched out on the floor and began doodling on one of the pads I had found in the end table.

A half hour later he began to move, but I didn't think anything of it until he bolt up in bed. Apparently my not being there had freaked him out a bit, until he swung his legs over the edge of the bed and spotted me at my spot on the floor.

"Morning." He yawned and stretched, casting an eye at me. "What are you drawing?"

"Just doodling really." I replied, tossing one of the granola bars up at him and looking back down at the giraffe I had begun to sketch, inspired by the one we had spotted last night. I guess it wasn't exactly at his own level of doodling because his mouth dropped open a bit and he moved closer to the pad, looking down at the sketch.

"That's not a doodle. That's actually pretty decent." I had to remind myself that it probably wasn't all that appropriate for me to continue staring at his chest and stomach, and moved my eyes back down to the pad. From someone else's standpoint I guessed it was pretty good, I hadn't worked at it very hard though. "You should go to an art school or something." At this I stifled a laugh and flipped onto my back so I could look up at him.

"That's kind of the reason I was looking forward to school. I was actually accepted into the university nearby, for art. Guess they found my doodles pretty decent as well." I winked, ignoring the feeling I got when I remembered that there would be no school for me, for either of us, until this mess was sorted out. "Not as big and fancy as the school downtown, but it's good enough for me." A choice that one or two of my friends had found ridiculous, you couldn't build a career on art as one of them had told me over and over. They made sure to try and puff up their school choices as much as possible in a last desperate bid to get me to change my acceptance and go to the more prestigious of the two schools. Sure my marks were good enough, had been good enough, but I just couldn't picture myself stuck behind some boring desk in a boring office, trapped in a life that followed the same strict set of rules that everyone else had to abide by.

"Wow, I didn't know that." He polished off the granola bar that I had tossed to him and wandered into the bathroom. Moments later I heard the shower turn on and I turned back to my pad, adding the cityscape behind the giraffe. When he was out and dressed, Mads and I were wrestling on the carpet. She was getting pretty antsy to go out, but there was no way in hell we were splitting up at this point, not if I had anything to do with it. "So, what's our game plan?" He cast a side-glance at the backpack that I had already packed, making sure that I hadn't left anything behind. "My guess is that we're going to head out and look around some more, try and find some answers?" I nodded and he grabbed his bag and dragged his clothes into the middle of the room, industrially folding and stuffing them haphazardly into the satchel. I had washed everything the night before and left them to hang on the edge of my radiator, they weren't dry enough to wear at this point, our jeans especially, but they were dry enough to stuff in the bags.

Soon enough everything was packed and Mads was clipped into her leash. We were ready to go and left the room, both of us checking the passageway for any signs of others. The gift shop presented a problem; neither of us were comfortable with the idea of leaving the man to starve to death, so Zach tossed one of the pocket knives that he had picked up the day before at the door and, making sure that the man knew it was there, added a few of our granola bars, an apple and some water to the pile. Neither of us spoke until we had left the building.

The giraffe was gone, something that surprised neither of us at this point. The day was spent in a more relaxed way than the day before. We talked and joked, not quite sure what we were doing at this point, instead walking around in a semi-daze that wasn't exactly productive. The one highlight of the day was spotting the zebras that ran as a herd down one of the streets, the three of us flattened against the wall of a brick building until they had passed. This meant, at the very least, that we weren't going insane and the giraffe last night was real. It also presented a bit of a problem that I had mentioned last night. There were more dangerous things in there than a few zebras or other gentle herbivores. The idea of a crowbar seemed better as the day wore on, and it wasn't even noon at that point.

We talked a lot, about our lives and the time we had spent together earlier in the summer before jobs and the like had split up our group until there were only the two of us, occasionally three whenever someone could get the day off, that were still hanging out on a regular basis. We laughed over the antics of some of our friends, recounting the time we had spent playing hide and seek in the cemetery like a bunch of terrified twelve year olds, the game eventually ending as the night grew on and more people frequented the grounds. It had been surprising, how many people wandered between the graves so late at night? Apparently quite a few. And we had all gotten spooked by the cop car that had pulled in, probably alerted by us dashing around. Now we both had a healthier respect for the dead, and weren't likely to go running around a cemetery any time soon. Granted, we hadn't meant any disrespect by it at the time.

The day wore on and we began strategizing whether or not to head back to the hotel for the night. I wasn't exactly excited with the chance that the man could have cut himself loose from his bonds by now, and the idea that he might be skulking around, just waiting for us to return, made me never want to step foot in there again. But we needed food at the very least, no sense in depleting our stores when we could just grab some stuff from one of the stores on our walk, and that was an easy enough decision to make at the moment.

"What's that?" Our reminiscing was stopped short when Zach grabbed my arm, stopping me in my tracks as both of us peered around an abandoned car. There were sounds coming from straight ahead. Human sounds. Creeping closer showed the shadowy figure of a man, standing stock still in front of a grocery store, eyes trained on the streets and back to the glass. The sounds weren't coming from him, but from the people who were presumably inside the store. Was he a lookout? My eyes went to the gun that flashed in the light of the sun and I decided that yes he was.

The allure of seeing people was winning against our caution. And besides, not everyone out there was evil. But just to be safe, and against my wishes, Zach decided to go first, toting Mads along for a small bit of extra protection. The last thing he wanted was to take a chance and put me in the crossfire of a weapon, and I bit my lip but stayed put like a good little girl. Mads was acting funny, barking under her breath and straining against the leash, trying to pull it from

Zach's grip and book it for the man who was standing guard. He noticed, sending a wary glance to Zach that I caught, having moved from my defensive position and crept closer to the lookout. Something in his stance, the way he moved and looked around, even stood, struck me as familiar. Eventually Zach was close enough that Mads eventually freed herself, pulling forth with a jerk that made him let go, and threw herself at the guard's legs with a whimper.

"Madigan?" The voice was surprised, as the man knelt swiftly to pat the dog, staring down at her in disbelief. "Mads. Calm down girl." He looked from Mads to Zach before casting his eyes around, possibly looking for someone else. "Who are you? This is my dog. She was with-"

By then I had already stood up, walking slowly to the man that just couldn't exist and nearly wanting to cry all over again. "Daddy?" The words escaped me when I was still metres away from the pair of them, but still close enough to see his face and be recognized in turn by him.

"Alice? Alice! Oh thank god." Next thing I knew, he had closed the steps between us and I found myself pulled into a giant hug as my father shook. I was too stunned to do anything but hug him fiercely back, not even noticing when Zach turned away to allow us our family reunion. "What are you doing here? I checked the house but you were gone, the both of you were gone, and I was afraid that..." His voice trailed off and he let me go, keeping one arm around my shoulder before turning back towards Zach. For his credit, Zachary was pretending to investigate a nearby sign and I remembered that this was something he was never going to get. It broke my heart a little, and I called out to him.

"Zach? Zachary, this is my father. Dad, this is Zachary." I introduced the two men, Zach offering his hand with a polite greeting of 'Sir' and a casual nod of respect which my father returned. "I stayed in the house for days waiting for you guys to come back, then I left and found him. We stayed at the hotel downtown for the night. Where the hell have you been?" My voice rose on the last sentence, a little bit of indignation creeping in. He could have called me! I had actively checked my cell phone to the point of it dying, it had a minimal charge on it from when we had been running the generator the night before, and it was enough to be checked a few more times. Not that there was any point to that at this time, except for one little thing. "Where's mom? Where's Katie? Are they all right?"

My dad breathed out a sigh when I had finished shrieking about the other half of our family and moved me to sit on the bench in front of the store, motioning Zach to do the same. "I'll start from the beginning. The police force was called in for some extra security for the event that was running down here a few days ago, or at least that's what they told us. Extra security my ass. One minute everything is fine and dandy, the next they're shuffling people into buildings with some obscure warnings. I sent your mom and Katie ahead, I knew I had to get you before I could go in, but everyone panicked and I couldn't get away. When I was on my way back the explosions started and I guess I was knocked unconscious for a bit. Next time I woke up there was no one in sight, and there were bodies everywhere from people who hadn't wanted to leave, whether they didn't believe in the threat or because they were trying to get back to people they had left at home. I went back to the house as soon as I could, but on the way I had a bit of trouble with a gang of men who were a little more rambunctious than usual. They were convicts, and a few of them recognized me as the cop who had put them behind bars. I was roughed up pretty bad and they left me to die. Tanner found me, and we both went back to the house but you and Madigan were gone. Since then we've been looking around for you, and anyone else really. We found Miranda yesterday morning, but no one else since then."

The people that I presumed my father was talking about had materialized from the grocery store, quietly standing near the entrance until my dad beckoned them over. The woman was striking, only a little bit older than Zachary and I, and her arm was in a sling. The man, Tanner, was around my father's age, seemed nice enough, and he looked from me to Zach with a small grin. Miranda, I noticed, seemed to only have eyes for Zach and I was stung by this.

"Miranda, Tanner, this is my daughter Alice and her friend Zachary. They'll be joining us, and I suggest that we head back home for now. It's going to get dark soon and those wolves I saw will make an easy meal of us if we're caught stumbling around in the dark." I looked up in surprise. So they had seen the animals too. Answering my unasked question, my father confirmed our theory that the earthquakes had brought down the walls of the zoo and, to my dismay, the prison walls as well. Those that had survived were now roaming the streets in packs or alone, and were both equally dangerous, man and beast alike.

My dad's mention of 'back home' made me wonder what he was talking about, especially because we weren't exactly following the route that would take the group back to our place. He lead the assembly, checking on me with sly glances every once in a while. Miranda and Tanner chatted amiably behind us, including Zach in the conversations every once in a while. I could tell that he felt a little misplaced; we had managed to fall into distinctive pairs, neither of which seemed to include him and I felt for him. Hopefully I would be able to shoulder off my dad's overprotective glances for a while, not that I didn't appreciate them, and make sure he was alright. The added fact that my father had appeared while his had been buried probably wasn't helping things along either. Eventually I realized I was brooding on these things and perked up, beginning to pay more attention to the route we were taking, both to attempt to determine where we were going as well as trying to memorize the course. With everything that had happened to us so far, there was no way in hell that I was going to be caught unprepared again. Not if I could help it anyways.

I almost stopped short when my dad lead us through some of the ritzier neighbourhoods of the city. In the back of my mind I had been expecting a public area like Zach and I had found in the hotel, or in the very least a place belonging to one of our relatives or a family friend. Nobody we knew lived in a place like this. To be honest, some of the garages we were walking past were larger than our home. Biting back my urge to question my dad I trekked along, losing a bit of ground so that I found myself walking beside Zach. Mads didn't exactly like this, she was taking the same kind of overbearing protectiveness over my father that she had exhibited with me after the attack, but I dragged her backwards with me and she didn't complain all that much. Before I had a chance to say anything to him, my dad stopped and turned back to face the rest of us.

We were standing in the driveway of one of the larger homes, its elegant walkway beckoning at us from behind an intimidating looking fence. It looked like the kind of thing that couldn't make up its mind, wanting us to visit and stay the hell away all at the same time. Still, beyond that gate was the kind of house that little girls dreamt about retiring to with their knights in shining armour. And we were turning up the driveway? How the hell did we expect to get into a place like this? The security on a million dollar home had to be just a little better than peanut shells on the floor or Vaseline on the doorknobs, which were the best features I could come up with. This was why I was going into art, instead of following in my dad's footsteps and becoming a cop.

Oh, with a passcode. Apparently my dad either had an in with the owner or he was just an excellent hacker. I wondered if he was grappling with the same moral conundrums that Zach and I had on our shopping spree, and maybe it was magnified for him because of his career choice. The thoughts carried me through the gate, watching as it whirred to a close behind us with a satisfying locking sound. It took me by surprise that the gate moved at all, even after only three days without electricity I had just assumed that, other than random generators that we would find, we'd be back in the age of the candle. Not that I was extremely disappointed to see that this place had electricity, it was reassuring in a way.

The winding path leading up to the doorway was shaded by large trees, and I bet that if there had been any sounds outside of the garden it would have been muffled, I couldn't picture a scenic area like this being harassed by a barrage of car noises and angry voices. The gate, sliding shut behind us with a smooth click, seemed secure enough to keep out whatever was still out there. I cast a wary glance at the top of the gateway, it didn't exactly look climbable and it was heartening that the likelihood of encountering the same kind of unwanted visitor that Zach and I had met in the hotel was slim to none. The house, looming before us like some kind of modern day castle, looked vacant.

Cole, my mind was already slipping back into my previous practice of referring to my father by his first name, unlocked the door and, after pausing in the doorframe to listen for a minute, ushered us inside. The interior was elegant, matching the image that my mind had conjured when we were still walking up the driveway.

It was all a little odd, and it took me several minutes to wrap my mind around everything that had and still was happening. Mom and Katie were safe, that was reassuring to a point. It sucked that Cole, my dad, didn't know Zachary or his family all that well, I would have loved for him to get some pleasant news about the whereabouts about his family, but all I could do at this point was check up on him every once in a while. Mentally of course, I doubted he would have appreciated me belittling him like that in front of these strange adults, treating him like a child. It probably would have messed with his macho-ness or some bullshit like that.

The group had dispersed without my realizing, leaving Zach and I standing awkwardly in the hall. Mads was straining against her leash, most likely trying to follow three different people at once and I quickly unclipped her and dropped her leash onto the banister where I could easily find it in the morning. "So what now?" He whispered to me, eyes looking everywhere at once.

"Well we should stay here for the night at least. I'll talk to my dad later, try to find out more about these people. But if he trusts them, so do I." And it wasn't like I wanted to leave my one relative in the world to go wander around aimlessly. We didn't have anything even close to resembling a plan. "Unless you're uncomfortable with staying?" He shook his head, as I had figured. "Alright, awesome. So we'll stay and do what they do." It was nice to have some kind of family type thing again, I hadn't realized before how cool that kind of thing was. It already felt homey, someone was making something in the kitchen, and the familiar click-click sound of Mads' nails on the wooden floor seemed right. Already I could feel myself becoming comforted, and the two of us wandered into the kitchen to see what was up.

Miranda was manning a pot on the stove, and I figured she was making some kind of spaghetti sauce, stirring the contents with her uninjured arm. Tanner was at the island, dutifully chopping vegetables that they must have gotten from the store. The windows were big and plentiful, and I could see into the fenced backyard that had a pool and a garden in a greenhouse. Hopefully there would be veggies or fruit in there. Things in the grocery stores weren't going to last for very long. "Need any help?" I asked shyly and was immediately put to work making garlic bread while Zach searched the pantry for a kind of pasta that everyone could agree on. We worked in a comfortable silence for the most part, with some casual conversation usually initiated by Tanner. He was curious, moreso than Miranda who seemed to either be ignoring the rest of us unless she was spoken to directly or really incredibly interested in her stirring technique.

Aside from the cold shoulder from our resident femme fatale (and I probably would only admit in my mind how much she got on my nerves) we were meshing... as well as could have been expected from a group of strangers. Dinner was quiet for the most part, Tanner had dragged out a novel and was reading at the table, Cole was absently shifting between a game of tic tac toe with Miranda and glancing at me, and Zach and I were taking turns tossing meatballs for Mads to catch.

"Dog food. We'll need to get some." My dad murmured, finally breaking the silence that had only previously been touched by the snapping sounds of Mads' teeth as she caught another piece of food.

"Yeah, we don't have that much left. Thankfully it should keep forever." Zachary held out his hand to the dog, and she curiously sniffed it in vain for more food before leaving a wet nose print and moving further along the table to search for crumbs. Nothing more was said, making me a little uneasy and I could see it in Cole's eyes as well. We were used to Katie's never ending muttering and her loud outbursts, or the way my mom could keep up a steady stream of chattering that was friendly enough to envelop anyone we had brought home with no fear of awkwardness. A slight tug at my heart, I both hoped they were okay and wondered how this was affecting Zach. For a while we had had something in common, but now I wasn't completely alone anymore.

Miranda's eyes had begun to droop before dinner was even cleared from the table, a side effect from the meds. Tanner nudged her and she put a bit of weight on him, stumbling off together towards the stairs that I had spotted on the way in.

"I usually turn the electricity off at night. Don't really want to broadcast our location. And the solar panels don't charge enough to keep everything going all night" My dad was wiping the table down with a rag, a burst of the setting sun burning red into the dark wood. "I know it's early still, but if you two want-"

"We're exhausted." I cut in, casually sidestepping any awkward glaring my father would do towards Zach in order to establish some clear-cut boundaries. "So if it's cool we're probably going to crash. Poor Mads, it's going to drive her insane going from room to room." Cole nodded, not much else he could do in the situation and shepherded us up the stairs.

"Usually Tanner sleeps on a cot in Miranda's room, she gets a little nauseous in the middle of the night and the medication can give her some pretty intense nightmares." I was surprised that my father had even managed to find the correct meds. That was more mom's area of expertise. Dad's belief was that if it could be covered with a Band-Aid, all was right in the world. "And I like to just sleep on the couch downstairs..." He opened one of the many doors along the hallway and I followed inside, dropping my bag on the bed. It had all of the personality of a guest room in a stuffy manor, but it would definitely do the job. "Zachary, you'll be down the hall." There was no missing that steel edge, my father was overreacting yet again. And he wondered why he had never really met any of my male friends.

I was alone for the first time that day, and I closed the door firmly while I got changed, Mads looking up at me with big eyes while I pulled a worn t-shirt over my head. "It'll be fine." I hadn't thought much about tonight; not that I had expected to stumble upon my father and his new 'roomies'. But not thinking about it during the day would hopefully lead to no nightmares, right? With an unnecessary cautious glance from side to side I dove into my bag, unearthing the small pill bottle I had grabbed while we were still a trio. Just one little pill, and I would be fine.

And so I slept.

Day 5

I have no idea what time I slept until, there wasn't really any clock in the room and my phone was so far dead that it would take a miracle and three days of charging to bring it back to life. It was a few minutes before I could even sit up; the previous few days had come rushing back to me and I was embarrassed to find tears on my cheeks. Mads was gone, someone must have opened my door to let her out. I sat up and forced myself out of bed. The bathroom was close, thank god, and I ducked in with relief after not seeing anyone milling about in the hallway. A cold shower and a change of clothes later and I was as ready to face the day as was possible.

Miranda and Zach were in the kitchen playing chess, the old wooden chessboard sitting between them. I thought Zach was winning but I had never been that great at the game. "There's cereal in the cupboard." He didn't look up, it was Miranda's move and she was busy taking his bishop with a black castle, knocking it out of the way with a grin.

I muttered my thanks, unearthing a bowl and spoon and eating standing up at the counter. The game was silent, both players repeatedly trying to find the weak spots in their opponent's defences. For a while it seemed like Zach was struggling, but he ended up taking her king with a defiant 'Checkmate!' and a cute half-smile.

As I had finished washing out my bowl and spoon and put everything in the dish rack, Cole came in with Mads trotting happily at his heels. "If you two are up to it, we'll be going out again today." The way he said it didn't exactly sound like we, or at the very least I, were being given much of a choice in the matter, but I was happy to allow my father to take the lead from now on. "We're trying to comb through the city sector by sector, see what we can find." I was glad to have something to do, and I could see that Zach was as well. We both desperately wanted to be helpful, and there could be nothing worse than hanging around the house and wondering about what had happened or whom we would never see again.

"Mads needs food." I reminded him, nudging the empty bowl that had served as hers with my foot. My dad passed me a list and a pen, I dutifully added my suggestion to the bottom and slid it back. He had always been mildly forgetful when it came to shopping. I figured that now was no exception. "Well, I'm pretty much ready to go." I knelt to fondle Mads' ears, eliciting that leg thumping tail wag she had recently developed. She was definitely getting bigger, her shape smoothing out to a more adult form and losing its previous puppy cuteness. For the umpteenth time I counted my lucky stars that I had her, she had been a huge help and my only companion for so many hours that it was hard to imagine her not being there.

We found ourselves outdoors again within the hour, Tanner having joined us from his gardening in the backyard. For the most part the walk was uneventful; the most exciting part being uncovering a flock of flamingos in one of the ponds that we passed by on our way deeper downtown. That was where we faced our first obstacle, an apartment building that could take all day to clean out.

"We should split up." Tanner advised, and I could see my dad tense out of the corner of my eye. It would make the most sense for him to go with Miranda and Tanner, she was next to useless with that arm, and leave Mads with Zach and me. But I knew that that was one of the last things he wanted to do. "It could take forever to check everything if we stay in a huge group. Going it alone would be the best," He paused and gave my dad a glance, obviously remembering his past experiences with the roaming gangs, "but obviously that's out of the question." A little backtracking and he was okay.

Against dad's wishes Zach and I took Mads to

the first floor. We were instructed to check for people first, and if things looked uninhabited to grab anything from the list I had dutifully copied out for each person. Then we would check in with them before moving onto the second, where we would all stay on the same floor and go apartment by apartment. I grabbed the heavy flashlight that Zach and I had taken from the hotel, holding it was comforting in a weird way. Aside from the fact that I knew it could do some serious damage to someone's skull, it was also nice to know that unless the battery failed I wouldn't be suddenly plunged into darkness. So here was to hoping that the batteries didn't spontaneously go through with some sort of warped murder suicide pact.

Dragging myself away from those less than happy thoughts, I schlepped along behind Zach. I wasn't going to be the first to admit that I was a little freaked out about what (or who for that matter) we could possibly find, but it was definitely the truth. The first few apartments were easily glossed over; one or two were even so far destroyed that we couldn't do much more than just barely poke our noses in where they probably didn't belong. Above our heads I could hear the rhythmic clomping of my dads boots, accompanied by the lighter quicker steps of Tanner and Miranda's awkward shuffle as she probably avoided glancing her arm off of something. "Thin walls, it must have completely sucked to live here. Especially if your neighbours were annoying people who blasted music day and night or had bratty kids." I remarked conversationally, effectively shattering the comfortable silence that had existed. Both Mads and Zach looked up in surprise, as if the pair had forgotten about my presence. Alright, so maybe I wasn't as intent as they were to find... whatever. But this place creeped me out, and I would be more than happy to have to leave. "At the very least we'll hear whatever's coming." I could feel an awkward tingling blush creep across my cheeks and darted into a bathroom just off of the main hallway. "I'll just look for... medical stuff. In here." My voice was weirder than I would have liked, it always cracked when I was super awkward. Kind of like a prepubescent boys. Definitely not my most attractive quality.

I made a fair amount of noise, following through with my garbled excuse by at least rummaging through the medicine cabinet. Nothing really useful unless I felt like prettying myself up with some makeup, and I let them clatter into the sink without really thinking about it. A bottle of medicine, the prescription label faded and watermarked to the point where it was almost ineligible. 'Nitroglycerine'. I loved the way medicine sounded when you spoke it, and the word rolled off of my tongue easier than my brain recalling my twelfth grade bio class. Blood thinners? I doubted it would be helpful, shouldn't really be taking someone else's prescription anyways. God only knew what other things lurked in that bottle, if it was even blood thinners that sat under the tightly closed cap was anyone's guess. So I haphazardly tossed those into the ceramic basin as well, shifting aside a few other bottles to peer around.

I heard something move in the bedroom right beside me, a dragging noise that scared me into freezing; one of the most useless defensive strategies ever developed into the human psychology. "Zach." My voice was hard to choke out and it was pretty close to silent. I heard Mads stop in her click-clacking walking, and I could almost imagine her tilting her head in confusion, trying harder to listen in. "Zachary." A little louder this time, but I could also hear the dragging noise again. What the fuck was that? "ZACHARY!"

Finally, my voice exploded out of my throat similar to the way he threw himself through the door, only milliseconds behind the blur that was Mads, all snarling teeth and puffed up fur. "Something, next room." I was shaking, I realized it when he grabbed my wrist and pulled me a bit closer, trying to shut me up so he could listen.

"Shhh." I could feel it reverberating through his chest, and I closed my eyes until the shivers stopped rippling through my frame. It took an embarrassingly long time, and I called myself stupid every inch of the way. I was prepared this time, I wasn't alone and I had that flashlight. I was going to be okay, we were going to be fine. Nothing bad was going to happen. "We're going to go in there, you'll be behind me and we'll let Mads go wherever. Hold on tight to the flashlight, swing at anything too close." I nodded, willing to let him take charge for once as my heart did rapid little rabbit beats in my chest, as if it was trying (and nearly succeeding) to escape. "C'mon." He let go of my wrist and sidestepped around me, threading one of my hands into a tighter grip around the flashlight as he passed. I clung to it like it was a life raft, my emotions sure felt like a churning dangerous sea. I'm sure my English teacher would have jumped all over that one, dissecting it to bits and pieces with symbolism this and imagery that, and not even left the poor girl that was Alice alone to lick her wounds.

I wasn't making sense again, and he was already two steps ahead of me. I scrambled to catch up, closing the distance between us until my nose was all but pressed into his back and he peered along the hallway. One door, it was closed and ominous looking, though now completely silent. My attention was drawn from the door to Zach's hand, which had risen to hover just in view over his shoulder. He was counting down, curling his fingers down from three, and by the time he reached one I had lowered my head and was charging in with him, Mads following along beside me with a strange whine.

We burst through the door, it flung open with the impact of Zach's body and he froze in the now empty doorway while I skidded to a stop behind him. I'm sure my eyes were wild and they darted around, I couldn't see much around my friend and I peered anxiously through the crook of his elbow, shuddering and taking a quick step back away from the corpse that was laying all splayed out on the bed not three feet from us. The smell hit us full in the face, and I instantly coughed and lifted my shirt over my nose, eyes watering against the stench. Blood was caked everywhere on the body, and was smeared along the walls as if she had tried to pull herself out of bed. "What the-" I couldn't even get all of the words out before we heard the shuffling again, a quick sliding of a body across hardwood floor that could only be coming from underneath the bed.

My mind instantly jumped to a ridiculous place, bed monsters and zombies that loomed in the darkness to tear apart our flesh and pluck our still beating hearts from cracked open ribs, a definite case of watching too many horror movies. Zach was cautious, grabbing a hold of the flashlight and dropping me down with him, a little jerk of the handle and I was crouched behind him, flashing it underneath the bed while he held onto the head of it to stop my shaking hands from skittering the beam everywhere. He was trembling too though; I could feel it from the way we crouched, my arm trapped under his while he fought to keep control.

Nothing could have prepared us for the child who crawled out from under the bed, all matted hair and big scared eyes. He was six or so, and shaking harder than either of us could possibly imagine. "What are you doing in here?" Zach's voice was as calm as he could manage, but you could still hear the break of emotion as he fought to keep the revulsion down. I was experiencing similar problems. How could this boy have hidden under what was presumably his dead mother's body? The sound of Zach's voice seemed to trigger the fight or flight instinct and he burrowed under the bed again, disappearing except for a pale face that glowed under the beam of the flashlight. "No, don't do that. We won't hurt you, we promise." I grabbed onto Mads' collar as she was straining to bound forward and sniff at the boy, and pulled her into me, wrapping my fingers into her thick fur. The boy skittered even further back, and we heard the audible thump as his body hit the wall on the other side of the bed. The body above shifted slightly as the bed vibrated, and it made my stomach lurch once more. At least her eyes were closed.

"C'mon kiddo, Zach's right." I found myself crab-walking forward, trying to forget about the human-like shell that was just above me as I scooted onto my hands and knees to peer under the bed. I could feel Zach right behind me, one hand wrapped protectively around my waist to… pull I guessed, in case this kid launched himself at my face or something. I doubted it would come to that, the tremors were cascading his body to the point where he could barely breathe. I could hear the oxygen being pulled into his body with short little gasps that couldn't have been helping his already addled brain. "We won't hurt you. My name is Alice, like Alice in Wonderland? You know the story?" My mind fumbled for a few lines of the Disney classic, and I muttered them to myself first to make sure I had them right. "Clean cup clean cup, move down move down?" If he didn't know it there was really no hope for this kid, and I had no other tricks up my sleeve. But Katie was around his age, and that kind of thing always worked on her. I could see his eyes get a little less weary, they softened a bit and one corner of his mouth turned up in a smile.

"That was mom's favourite, she loved the Mad Hatter." He muttered quietly to himself, almost unconsciously sliding out a bit. He seemed to realize what he was doing and pulled his hand back from the spot where it had been reaching out to me, cradling it to his chest and whimpering quietly once or twice before subsiding into silence.

Zach and I followed suit, sitting as patiently and quietly as we could. Mads even laid herself down, head on Zach's leg and I could feel my own legs cramping under the steady loss of blood to my ankles. I wavered a bit, trying not to fall into the puddle that leeched down through the sheets and was suspiciously dark like blood.

It seemed ages before the boy slid out, avoiding looking at the prone body above him, and buried his face in my chest. It may have been inappropriate at any other time, but as it stood I enveloped him in the tightest hug I could manage without cracking any of his little bird-like bones and rocked him until the wracking sobs subsided and his breathing became a little less normal. He still flinched when Zach patted him awkwardly on the shoulder, but not as much and at the very least he pressed himself into me. Apparently I was now Alice, Lord Protector of this boy's fragile sense of reality and it was a job I took dead serious. He reminded me more and more of Katie, her eyes were close to that shade of green, and her nose did that cute little button thing that I had been so jealous of when I was fifteen and stupid.

We stayed where we were for a few more minutes, only moving into a more wildly protective stance when we heard the heavy thumping footsteps drawing rapidly closer until the door banged open again, I hadn't realized that we had closed the front door behind us, and we could hear my father's frantic calling of my name. Zach answered and Cole essentially ran into the room, nearly tripping over Mads who had leapt up to wag her tail happily over the odd picture in front of him. "What in the name of-" but I had stood up, the boy piggybacking with arms firmly clasped around my throat and one of Zach's hands on his shoulder.

"Dad, no. Not now. I'll explain later. I've gotta get him out of here." I could see my dad's eyes widen, possibly at the sight of the bloodied figure on the bed, but he let me pass with a wordless nod, keeping his distance from the once-again shuddering child on my back. Tanner and Miranda were standing in the hallway, apparently torn between following Cole's mad rush to find me and preferring the safer route of not getting in his way should we not have been in that apartment. Both of them made to speak when they saw my koala-kid, but a warning glance from both Zach and Cole made Tanner at least shut up, though Miranda's mouth was still gaping open like a fish. As much as I wanted to stop and enjoy the sight I stomped past, clutching at the kids legs. He was light as a feather, and I wanted him out of this place as fast as possible. It had to have been a million times worse for him than it had been for Zach, god only knew how long he had stayed in that apartment with his mother's rotting corpse. I wanted to shower, who knew how dirty this poor child felt?

I was three buildings away before anyone but Mads had caught up with me. I had to admit, I was pretty driven in my blind need to get him somewhere safe and clean and warm. Even the repeated callings of my name hadn't managed to snap me out of things, though when I was a block away I realized that they had all fallen into step behind me, my father at my side and scouting the way in a characteristically cop-like manner.

We were home faster than when we had come out, and everyone stood around awkwardly in the hallway while I sat the kid down at the table, prying his iron grip from around my neck and ushering Mads over to lay her head in his lap. He clung to the dog while I rummaged through the fridge before getting frustrated and going to where the kid-friendly food had to be. The cupboards were easy, I spied one of those easy to make macaroni things that could glow orange even in the dark and made myself busy, plopping a full bowl in front of him when it was done. No one had said anything, but I could hear my dad and Zach talking quickly and quietly in the next room over. I neither knew nor cared where Tanner and Miranda had skulked off to, but after a while I heard the door quietly shut and Zach came into view, shrugging off his backpack and setting the flashlight that I had cast aside mid-hug on the table. "They've gone to finish up, there's a store nearby that they can pick through. Nobody wanted to be gone long."

I nodded, both of us turning to the sounds of eating as the kid demolished the bowl I had put in front of him, even going so far as to scrape the cheese off of the sides with his fork. I stood and got him another full bowl, setting it in front of him and backing off as Zach found him a juice box. We repeated the process as necessary, refilling until the kid's eyes drooped and his head nodded against the table. It was then that I risked the only question anyone really needed to know at that point in time. "Hey buddy, you have a name? You know mine and Zach's, and that's Madigan in your lap. But we don't know yours." I hoped he was lulled off into sleep enough to not tense into himself again, and I was right. He managed a sleepy reply of "Trent." before folding his arms on the table and setting his head into them. We gave him a few minutes, to make sure he was completely zonked out before Zach moved him up into his room, he would crash somewhere else until we figured everything out.

Feeling drained, I trooped off to the couch near the big bay windows, both waiting for the return of everyone else and desperately wanting to sleep myself. Zach and I talked for a while, I honestly couldn't tell you what about, and I fell asleep embarrassingly soon, though a quick glance at the clock had told me it was getting on in the evening. I could feel Zach settling in beside me, and I didn't think twice about burrowing in beside him, taking comfort in the warm living boy who sat next to me on the couch.

My peaceful sleeping wasn't interrupted by their return like Zach's was, and he was up and off of the couch before they had even come through the door. I didn't even notice him leaving, and he told me that I slept through them offering me a plate of leftover pasta, and even their conversation in the dining room right next door. What I woke up for was when it got loud and scary, and the three bottles of wine that lounged near the stairs attested to how bad it could get. Tanner and my father were engaged in a heated shouting match, Miranda was nowhere to be found and Zach was hovering in between the two men, presumably to stop it from getting ugly. Apparently Tanner had imbibed a little too much, who even knew where he had unearthed the alcohol from, and was threatening to throw the boy - Trent - onto the streets.

"We can't afford a child, he'll fuck everything up! He's not like these two, he can't help out. He's a risk, we shouldn't have brought him here!" His words were slurred and he stumbled a bit though he hadn't taken a step, and suddenly I was bolt upright on the couch. I was in between the stairs and Tanner, and as soon as my father returned his comment with harsh words of his own and Tanner took those threatening few steps towards the staircase I booked it up the stairs, falling a bit in my sleep dredged stupor. Heavy footsteps followed behind me, and I heard him hit the ground at one point, probably falling over himself on the steps like I had. But his mistake was alcohol induced, he was slower than me and I was running on pure adrenaline. I flung open the door to Zach's room and slammed it quickly behind me; I could hear the thudding sound of a body hitting the wood and my own reverberated with the impact, my back against the door to keep the insanity out.

Trent was sitting up in bed, the covers tangled around his shoulders as his little face peeped out, eyes wide like when we had found him. He was shaking again, and tears were apparent in the redness of his eyes and the streaked grime marks along his cheeks. Another thump, I held the doorknob firmly in my hand as he tried unsuccessfully to rattle it and dislodge the lock. Then I heard a grunt, Tanner's, and a woman's voice that spoke along with my dads. Cole and Miranda were leading him away, I could hear their voices growing fainter as they calmed the angry drunk down, and I moved away from the door in an uncharacteristically fluid motion, sliding into the bed and pulling Trent into my lap. Every so often there was another futile thump at the door, and I heard the lock click, which was followed by more angry screaming and threats and more calming down. I covered Trent's ears, rocking him again in my lap and humming, anything I could do to stop him from hearing what was going on downstairs.

The door creaked open. My eyes instantly went from the shadowy figure at the door to Mads who had bolted inside to stand guard at the base of the bed. I was about to move Trent behind me, block him with my own body, when Zach stepped into the light and shut the door behind himself. He locked it, probably better than I had in my panic filled actions, and set a chair up under the knob so it couldn't be popped open again. Then he slid into bed with us, his arms around my waist as I began to rock Trent again. I don't know how long we stayed like that; though it was definitely long enough for Trent to fall back into an uneasy sleep, the time seemed to stretch for miles.

Things were quiet downstairs except for the distant rumblings of talking and I felt Zach nod off, his chin resting on my shoulder. I sat like that for even longer, leaning slowly back so that he was leaning against the headboard and I could lean back against him, dragging Trent along with me.

There would be no need for sleeping pills tonight.

Day 6

It was quiet when I woke up, sleepy tendrils of bright sunlight stretching their way across the covers that had originally been wrapped around Trent. I had no idea how I had managed to be trapped in them as well, nor did I know exactly how we had managed to sleep parallel to one another, all of us in a neat little row with the sleeping child sandwiched protectively between us. Mads had sprawled across the foot of the bed, she was probably the reason that my legs were asleep and my feet were tingly with pins and needles. I dislodged the dog, causing her to look up at me with disdain before settling back into sleep. She looked older, though I guessed we all did with everything that had happened in the past few days. Some of the puppy-ness was gone, lost to a more slender fierce looking dog that I didn't quite know.

A little rattled, I moved out of the bed, sliding neatly out without causing any more than a mumble and some shifting from my fellow bed partners. I wanted to shower but I was afraid to open the door. It sat cold and frightening against the far wall, glaring at me in a way that only an ominous door could. It knew that I desperately needed to pee and was mocking me for being afraid. Unwilling to be bested by an inanimate piece of wood I stepped forward and lightly pressed my ear against the door, listening for a few seconds before dropping down on my hands and knees to peer underneath. I couldn't see or hear anything so I figured that it was safe to go out and I moved the chair from underneath the knob, sliding it quietly across the hardwood floor.

No one was outside of the door; no lurking traps or snarling faces so I figured it would be safe to pee. A few quick steps and I was in the bathroom, and I didn't hear anyone move even after I was done. It was still wicked early, I didn't have a watch so I could only guess that it was around seven in the morning. Figuring that the nap had helped in my sleeping pattern I moved downstairs, prepared to gather up some food and dash back upstairs before anyone noticed. I didn't encounter anyone until the kitchen, where Tanner was passed out on the table, his head in his arms. Stifling a harsh word or two that I knew would surely start up his hangover, I remained quiet and went along with my original plan. A box of cereal was in my hand and some fruit in the other when he started to wake up and peered at me with ashen face and red eyes.

"Save it." I snarled, watching as his lips attempted to form some kind of half assed apology. "And stay the fuck away from him or I swear to god I'll gouge out your eyes and feed them to you." I slammed the bowl of fruit back into the fridge and watched his wince with a satisfied smirk. It was nice to not have to take care of the drunken idiot, the babysitter role being one I usually played when my friends and I had gotten a little wild. "You'd better apologize though, or find some way to not make him take off in the middle of the night. I'm not going to babysit you Tanner, and you made a big mistake." It was a bit odd, normally I wasn't this aggressive and I sure wasn't used to having an adult take me this seriously. It was kind of nice.

He didn't try to say anything else and instead settled into a morose silence, watching as I moved from cupboard to cupboard in search of some glasses. Arms laden down with food I shot him another warning glare and moved away, an eerie prickling feeling scattering down my neck when I turned my back on him. I was still a little uneasy apparently, but he was dangerous and had irrefutably proven that last night. I wasn't going to cut him some slack because he couldn't control himself when he was under the influence. Drunken actions are sober thoughts after all.

They still weren't awake when I came back, which presented a bit of a problem with the juice but I couldn't do more than stash it on a chair and hope it wouldn't be too warm before they woke up. Now that the rush of adrenaline from confronting Tanner had left me I was a little bored and there was nothing to do about it besides ruffling Mads' ears and rolling myself up in a discarded blanket on the floor like a burrito. I was still in this ridiculous position when they woke up, Trent first with furtive glances around the room as if he had forgotten where he had fallen asleep the night before. I saw the momentary well of emotion that threatened to break and send him into hysterical crying, but he was a trooper and held those tears back. Zach woke with a grumble, tossing and turning had apparently not prolonged his sleep and the sun was now aimed full force directly into his eyes. I didn't blame him for the crankiness, even though he wasn't fully awake yet I could sympathize.

I carefully skidded the chair across the floor until it was within reach of the bed. Trent swung his body around until his legs dangled over the edge, feet swinging several inches above the floor. Kid was tiny. It struck me how young he must be, my previous guess had probably been younger than he actually was but he was still a baby in comparison to the rest of us. "How are you feeling, better?" I pushed the hair out of his sleep encrusted eyes, tucking it as close to behind his ears as I could while tutting quietly. I hadn't exactly pegged myself for the mothering type, but this little boy had no one left in the world and the least I could do was be a little compassionate.

"Yeah." His little voice was so tiny, and I knew he would send a few of my child-loving friends into ditzy swoons. I had had enough to deal with Katie and had never understood the mothering instinct. I guess it took a few disasters to bring out those unnoticed qualities of yourself. "That man doesn't want me here."

So he had heard what transpired downstairs, and understood it enough to know he should be afraid of the words and not just the shouting. "Well, we aren't going to listen to him. And as long as you're with me you're safe, you got that? Nobody is going to send you away, you're ours now." I waved my hand at the sleeping figure of Zach, groggily starting to wake up and look at us.

Trent nodded, obviously seeming unsure about my words but trusting me nonetheless. "Now eat your breakfast, and we'll figure out what's going on downstairs. My dad will know what we're doing today, he's a police man after all." How could those words not seem impressive to an eight or whatever year old? To Trent's credit, he seemed like an intelligent little boy but he was just that, a child in a world that he couldn't even begin to understand. Hell, I couldn't understand it myself.

Pouring two cups of the juice and offering Zach the rest of the bottle, the three of us sat in silence until Mads began her incessant whining and it was clear that people were beginning to move around downstairs. Trent's face closed up, obvious fear written across it and I turned to him to reassure him once more that nothing was going to happen to him. "C'mon little man, we've gotta start the day and show those adults that you're even braver than they are." He nodded and jumped off of the bed, Zach following with a stretch and a yawn.

Mads was first down the stairs, claws clicking on the hardwood comfortingly as Trent pressed his tiny hand into mine. I took it and gave it a reassuring squeeze, leading him to the dining room table where my father sat quietly conversing with Miranda. Tanner was nowhere to be seen and I was glad, there was no reason to terrify the kid any more and I wanted my dad to be the first adult he saw. Cops were comforting after all.

"First order of business sir?" I asked, trying to make my tone as pleasant and pleasing as possible. Like I hadn't threatened one of our group just hours before. "Though if I may, I suggest a proper first introduction is order. Trent, this is my dad Cole and Miranda, one of our friends." I doubted that Miranda would play nice, our earlier interactions hadn't proven her to be an extremely friendly person to me at least, but I had more hope for my father.

"Charmed." Surprisingly, Miranda was the perfect picture of friendliness and shook Trent's miniscule hand in a way that made him smile shyly. So it was just me she hated, though I bet if I had been a male she would have tried her feminine wiles on me as well. Cole shook his hand too, and I almost wished he still had his uniform on to make him seem that much more officer-like. Maybe it had just been growing up with a cop for a father, but there was something about the police force that made me feel a bit safer.

"We're going to try and piece some things together today." He said, nodding a hello to Zach who had just wandered out of the kitchen with an apple in hand. "Try to figure out what happened and where everyone has gone. Figure out what to do next." I could see that he wanted to leave Trent at home, probably with me as a guardian but there was no way in hell I was going to be left behind again. If it meant I'd have to carry the boy on my back I would.

"Makes sense. And with all of us going we can reach out a little farther." Maybe I sounded a bit harsh, but I was trying to get a point across. And if Miranda was allowed out, Miranda with her stunning looks and her broken arm, then there was no reason to leave a fully capable me at home to twiddle my thumbs and wait for the men to come home.

"We can try and gather a few more things too, no sense in wasting a trip." Zach added, swallowing the last of the apple and thankfully ignoring the eyes that Miranda was making at him. Either he was blissfully oblivious or had no interest. To be honest I was hoping for the latter.

"I suppose that makes sense." I could see it in my fathers eyes that he didn't want to agree with me but also didn't have the energy to pursue a fight. "We need to keep looking for survivors, have to help in any way we can. And it's important that we find out what happened, and why no external support has been radioed in." He was uncomfortable with no backup, and it made no sense to the rest of us either. Why had the police force from neighbouring places been so quiet and slow to respond? Had they been hit with whatever that we were facing as well? The questions seemed to be floating around the room, leaving Trent more or less unaffected as he busied himself with tugging at Mads ears in an attempt to get her to pay attention to him. Her tail thumping along the floor was the only soft sound for a long moment before we all decided to ask the unanswered question.

"What about the twerp?" Miranda, who was sitting closest to him, nudged Trent with a leg in a friendly manner. "It's probably not safe to leave him here, but who knows what we're going to find out there." Cole nodded, apparently in complete agreement with the latter. We couldn't leave him here, as I was unwilling to play the babysitter. I knew that was what he was thinking, as my father turned to me with that look he always had when he knew I wouldn't comply with what he had asked immediately.

"Well Alice could-" He was interrupted by Miranda, and for once I didn't hate what came out of her mouth. "I wouldn't have a problem staying with him. My meds are killing me anyways, and I would just slow you guys down." My father wore the face of someone who knew he was outnumbered. I knew it frustrated him to no end to bring me along, but I was an adult dammit and fully capable of making my own decisions. While Miranda wasn't exactly who I had in mind to watch Trent, I didn't really see the harm in her napping or whatever while he puttered around to keep himself entertained. It was unlikely that I would have to worry about him leaving the house on his own. I doubted he would ever leave again unless I asked him specifically to do so.

"Does that sound like a good plan little man?" Not wanting to leave him out of the decision, I kneeled down and made sure he knew what I was asking. "Are you okay with Miranda staying here with you while the rest of us go out there and bring home some dinner?" If there was one thing I knew about children it was to appeal to their stomach. I was kind of the same way, it was a bond we shared. Trent didn't like it, but I also kind of figured that he didn't like disappointing me either and was willing to let things slide for just this one time. He nodded, but barely made eye contact with anyone else in the room. Miranda was probably the least threatening after Zach and I and it was kind of my only option if I wanted to play with the big boys. "Perfect, that's my boy. I'll see if I can find you some colouring books or something to play with!" He would still like colouring books right? Or was that a girl only thing?

Our roles decided, we each set out to prepare and gather our wits and our backpacks. I settled Trent in with Miranda, drawing some quick sketches that he could fill in with the few coloured pens I had managed to find in a drawer as well as leaving him the pad with some instructions to draw some things for me to decorate our room with. There was no question that this little tadpole would be sleeping with me until we could get things sorted out or he could be saddled with Zach. Zach was busy making everyone sandwiches and snacks for the road, and it was kind of cute how easily he slipped into the role of mom. I watched him for a moment, worried he would look up and catch me looking at him, grateful once again that I had a friend to ride this whole thing out with. And a father too, it was nice to have an adult to lean on when things got a bit too much to handle.

Though I knew this city like the back of my hand, I still felt unsettled when we passed through the gate and waved our goodbyes to the tiny figures standing in the window watching us leave. There was a nagging feeling in my stomach, and I knew there would be until I returned home to make sure my boy was okay. No that I didn't trust Miranda, but I just didn't trust her. Who could trust someone who played people that easily without them ever realizing it? All I could do was take comfort in the fact that someone was watching him and stick with my assigned group of my father. We wouldn't split up until we absolutely had to, but it had been discussed amongst the men that Tanner and Zach would take Mads and I would stick with Cole if anything ever happened. Being the only person with a gun probably made my father the leader, and it didn't help my feeble arguments against the idea. I'd have to get my hands on a bat or something sooner or later, I didn't need anyone looking at me like I was vulnerable and in need of constant protecting.

The streets were quiet until we hit the downtown core, where the smell of corpses was most tear inducing. We had decided to visit city hall first, hoping to find some clues as to what was going on or at least someone who was in charge and cowering in the secured building. Keeping our eyes peeled for anything that would help in the who knew how long we would be stuck here, the animal spotting's were skyrocketing in a noticeable way. Where Zach and I had only seen the solitary giraffe before, we were now assaulted with strange birdcalls and flashes of fur as they darted amongst the streets. I half hoped that we wouldn't find anything too vicious, but I still held onto the childlike dream that I could possibly tame something and use my animal empathy to build an army.

As much as I would have liked to command my own pride of lions, I was skittish and jumped at anything that knocked over a trashcan. The city was getting quieter as we moved towards our destination, and I wondered if it was a bleak sense of disappointment that had settled over us instead of any environmental changes. What would we find when we entered the building? And would we even be able to decode it.

"Security seems pretty lax." I quipped, breaking the silence and making Tanner jump. It was true though, the booths inside were empty and there was no sign of any power feeding the scanners. "I'm just glad I won't have to take off my shoes and empty out my pockets." I caught a half smile from Zach and was glad that my humour was not going completely unappreciated. "But in all seriousness, we aren't the major center of the country. What are the chances we're going to find any information?" What could our tiny mayor possibly know that would help us? Our biggest city event was the farmers market that happened every summer. It was kind of a boring place.

"We might find something. And any answer is important right now." My father, ever the voice of reason, steered us to the mayors office first. We hadn't spotted anyone yet and the two filing cabinets in the room didn't seem that promising. "We'll take the desk, you guys each take a cabinet."

Sorted into our tasks, I ruffled through the few papers I found in the first drawer. Family portraits littered the top of the desk and what I was doing felt scarily intrusive. Nothing of interest caught my eye, just financial statements and receipts for invoices.

Apparently nobody else had found anything useful either, as there was silence and the soft sound of paper being tossed around. No sense in being careful if there was nobody around to complain about the mess.

"I've got something about testing." Tanner's voice was the first to break the spell, and we all froze as he skimmed the folder in his hands. "Scheduled testing that matches the date of the explosions, but nothing about evacuations or sirens or deaths." I glanced at Zach, he was quiet in his spot on the floor, though I could see him pale at the idea that his father's death may have been due to some routine testing or maintenance or whatever it was. That it had been planned. "Some chemical compounds, but nothing I remember from any Chemistry class I ever took." He passed them along to Zach, who shook his head and skipped right over me to hand to my father. Everyone knew I was a lost cause; those two years in Bio had left me with little to no knowledge about anything with numbers. Ask me to dissect a pig and I was all over that, but please don't ask me to explain something I can't even see.

"This is a good start." Cole carefully slipped the papers into a bag he had found, dumping a few more into the bag a few moments later. "We should move on. Gather anything that looks important, we can always come back or look them over at home." It made sense; we had a lot of ground to cover getting supplies and everything before dark. Not knowing what was out there, but we knew there was some reason not to hang around at night, was akin to the feeling you had as a child. Things that went bump in the night was apparently a feeling that could haunt you forever.

It didn't take long for us to finish emptying out the filing cabinets, and we remained uninterrupted as we left the building. Outside, the same eerie silence permeated everything. It was so unsettling, seeing places that were never devoid of people empty and lifeless. Only a few crows circled overhead, some picking at the occasional body we saw among the streets. "Should we do something about them?" I asked Cole quietly, remembering the impromptu service we had held for Zach's father when it was still the two of us. "They're gonna start to smell. And it's just not... right to leave them out like this. It's undignified." I didn't know what we could do about it. The idea of digging graves for all of these people was completely unappealing. Even a mass grave would have to be huge, and moving the bodies would be tricky.

"We could consider burning them." Cole answered, eyes scouting the road ahead. The mall was our next stop, as we had all agreed that now we had found our maddeningly small amount of information we should stock up on supplies. "But it's a lot of work and we would still keep finding them. We can just say a quick prayer and hope that nature takes care of them." It wasn't a kind thought, but probably the best one. We didn't have the manpower to deal with the crowds of dead.

"Dad, what about mom and Katie? Shouldn't we be focused on getting to them? I'm sure wherever they are they have food and it would be a whole lot safer." I could see my dad visibly tensing, but it wasn't a question we could avoid forever. He seemed to pause forever, clearly searching for his words before he carefully answered me.

"I tried to get back to them, once Tanner had patched me up. But there's no way in. They're at Sherbrooke station, I watched them go in with the rest of them. I watched them walk past the guards with rifles, getting as many people in there as they could. I watched them go in, but I can't get back to them. They've shut everything down, and aren't letting anyone else in. They're just refusing entry, and I had to get back to you. Once everything's settled down they said, whatever the hell that means. I guess they're safer in there, officials are always notoriously slow to get organized so I guess I shouldn't be surprised that we're not getting any answers yet." He seemed complacent; like he was willing to wait for those answers and as long as my family was safe I was going to do the same. After all, what could I do besides follow his lead? He definitely had more of an idea of what was going on than I did.

"So we're going to just leave them in there? Why won't they let the rest of us in? Or let them out?" That part was baffling to me. Organized or not, it was just time, money and food that they were expending to keep them in and us out. Was there something out here that we should worry about? Or something in there? I made a mental note to not let this sit for long, to try and figure out what was going on in this chaotic place we called home. Not that I figured I could determine very much at all. I was just a prospective art student, not Nancy Drew.

"I couldn't tell you." Cole went silent, obviously grappling with his own silent demons. It was apparent that he wasn't as okay with this as he was letting on, it was probably just some way for him to make me feel a little bit better about the whole situation. A little more normal. I let it slide, we had reached the mall and I was determined to get a few changes of clothes and to pick up some new things for Trent. A toy or a colouring book or something, anything to keep him occupied.

Maybe one of those math books that you worked on when you were little, racing through each page to get to the end and feel a little smarter about yourself.

I stuck with my father like he had instructed me to do. We would go through the stores one by one, skipping whatever we deemed unnecessary as a group and canvassing the rest in pairs. Zach and Tanner wandered off as soon as we hit the first major department store, each of them equipped with their own lists to try and fulfill whatever they were seeking out. I managed to grab a few things for Trent, not locating the workbooks I had wanted to keep his mind busy, but settling for a few crosswords and a colouring book with some crayons. The 64 pack, the one that made you the most popular kid in preschool. Especially if it had the sharpener in the back, like this one did. "Stuffed animals, stuffed animals…" I muttered under my breath, aware that Cole wanted to move on but still understood my purpose in this section.

It took a while, I wasn't exactly the champion of buying toys for children and I'm terrible at reading signs. Finding the aisle I wanted, I scoped out some of the cuddliest big ones and settled on a dog that looked similar enough to Mads to hopefully make him feel safe. Hell, she helped me. Even just hearing that familiar click-clack of her nails on any hard surfaced floors was enough white noise to make me think of home and feel slightly more comfortable. The dog went into the bag, and I felt a bit like a kid in a candy store. Ignoring prices was a bit difficult to do, but we all knew that there was really no point in leaving any money. Not that it was that useful to use either.

I tried to ignore Cole's raised eyebrows at my choice of weapon, the heavy wooden baseball bat feeling sturdy in my hands. "What? You have a gun." I pointed out, giving it a test swing and figuring I was unlikely to find anything better. With that and the knife I had slipped into my pocket, I felt fairly confident in maintaining my own safety and applauded my choices. Guns were out of the question, I didn't have the first idea of where to find one. I was a fairly decent shot, my father had instilled in us very early on with a healthy fear and respect of those metal boom-sticks. There was also no way in hell Cole would trust me with one, he'd probably be worried about me shooting off my own foot or something ridiculous.

Zach and Tanner had surveyed the prescription aisles, scoring us some much needed medicine. The idea of Miranda getting worse, or healing incorrectly even set me on edge, and she wasn't exactly my favourite person to have around. Nobody even really knew what to give her, so we were stuck with collecting a ton of bottles that we were only vaguely familiar with the names of. I quickly glanced over the pile, to see that tiny familiar bottle I had been so dependent on while I was just with Zach, but it wasn't there. Probably for the best, I would have to learn to sleep without any medication, nightmares or not.

Medicine and toys aside, we made our last stop in a clothing store, bypassing the one I wanted in favour of warmer, sturdier clothes. Our relatively quiet chatter was more muffled as we spread out more, each taking on their own responsibilities and feeling more comfortable since nothing had happened while we were here. I felt a bit better; the bat was a comforting weight against my back, nestled snugly in my backpack within easy grabbing range. I saw that Zach and Tanner had both had similar thoughts. Tanner had a hunting knife hooked onto his belt now, and Zach had taken the same smashing route as I had but his choice lay with a hammer. Less reach, but probably a bit more dangerous and definitely more useful in a day-to-day context.

I rifled through a few racks, tossing a pair of jeans that I was pretty sure would fit and a hoodie into my backpack. A few t-shirts and I would feel clean enough every day. I didn't want to grab too many, who knew how soon things would be figured out, but it was pretty necessary to me not to get too ripe. It would lower team morale or something. A few pairs of underwear made their way into the bag, along with a bra I had had my eye on for a while anyways. My own shopping done, I headed into the children's section to take care of Trent. Mads brushed up against my leg, leaning her full weight on it for a moment before moving on. She was given free reign now, nobody expected her to go running and it was nice to let her wander around a bit. She was smart enough to let us know if anything wrong was afoot.

Trent was easy. Little boy clothes were made to take a lot of wear and he seemed like the kind of kid to appreciate shirts with race cars on them. A pair of shoes, his seemed to have seen better days, and a couple more things and I was almost done. An odd rumbling seemed to permeate nearby, but I chalked it up to some kind of air conditioning or heating system rumbling it's last dying breaths and didn't pay much attention to it. Last stop, underwear and boy was it a little awkward. Little boy underwear wasn't exactly my forte, but I wasn't willing to expose my discomfort to Zach and give him the task. He looked interested enough in whatever he was doing as it was. Mads kept pacing in front of the aisle, blocking my access and I gently nudged her out of my way. The rumbling increased, and I realized that it was coming from the dog. Teeth bared and hair standing up along the ridge of her back, I was surprised to see Mads in full on attack mode. The rumbling intensified into a growl, and her lips curled up even further. "Madigan, what's your deal?" Nobody had entered the store since we had, and we had a pretty clear view of the door. I doubted that anyone was hiding among the racks we hadn't already combed through, though I guessed it was possible. "Dad?" I called out, slowly drawing the bat from my backpack and standing, unsure of where to look. Cole was at my side in moments, eyes going to Madigan before scoping the area.

"Did you see anything?" I shook my head no, neither of us knowing exactly where to search. I could hear Zach and Tanner nearby, alerted to our interest and slowly stepping forward to join the ranks. Sensing that the need for quiet was imperative, no one said a word and all eyes were on the dog as she slowly inched her way towards the aisle I had made my next mission. A new rumbling joined in, one that I wasn't so sure was coming from Mads. It was deeper, gravelly and something I couldn't quite place. Cole stepped slightly in front of me, gun drawn and pointed a few steps before Mads.

One of the stands erupted in a explosion of folded boxers. A streak of gold landed near Mads, running at her and taking the form of a lioness. I stifled a gasp, stepping forward to grab at Mads collar and pull her back but I was stopped by Cole lunging forward, firing a round with his gun that missed by inches. The beast took a running jump, swiping at man and dog and managing to hit both before I knew what was really happening. My brain was in overdrive, adrenaline pumping through my veins and I was barely aware of what was going on anymore.

My hands hurt, and I realized that I had moved to brandish my bat as the weapon I knew it would be. The vibrations made my hands shake, and I immediately dropped the bat due to the recoil of connecting with such a solid object. I had hit a lion. In the face. With a bat. What in the hell.

The gun had skittered to the side and my father had dropped, so I lunged for it. Though stunned, natural instincts took in and the lioness went after me, clipping the back of my leg and I crashed to the ground. I could hear screaming and realized it was my own, but also knew that the gun was in my hand. The cool metal felt familiar, and I drew it in front of me and timed my breathing just like Cole had taught me.

I couldn't be distracted with how anyone else was doing, as the most terrifying sight I had ever experienced barrelled down on me with long white fangs exposed. One shot, and then another, and the heavy weight dropped onto my legs.

There was silence, only broken by Mads utterly heartbroken cries of pain as she tried to drag herself to me. I reached out to her, feeling the tingle of fur as it brushed against my outstretched fingertips. My leg was already a nearly forgotten sting, the circulation being cut off actually helping. Or so my woozy brain told me.

"Leave it on her." I could hear my father, thank god he was okay. There was blood on my chest, and it took a while to realize it was from the bullet hole I had put into the back of the lions head. Hand firmly entangled in Mads fur, I heard the dispute while they argued. At first it didn't make sense, and then I figured out that they would want to keep the weight on until they could get their wits and their bandages together to staunch the bleeding as quickly as possible. "Grab those gauze pads and the hydrogen peroxide." He had been the one we always went to whenever we got banged up or scratched, though his previous attitude for just slapping a Band-Aid on something seemed to have been scrapped for a more logical approach. Mom kissed the ouches better, dad was the one who fixed them up.

"No no no no no not that." I watched as they uncapped the chemical, knowing the searing pain that was waiting for me. "It barely hurts, I can't even feel it." I was shushed and someone grabbed my hand, squeezing it while the weight was unexpectedly lifted off of my leg. The pain returned, a harsh throbbing that made my eyes water and a whimper involuntarily leave my lips. So much for being strong. The bottle was tipped over my leg, foaming and turning pink in the blood that was beginning to return. I muffled a yelp, biting into the collar of my shirt as I had managed to finagle it into my mouth. The bandage they wrapped around it stung even more, the rough fabric chafing against the ragged edges of the broken skin. I let go of the hand I was holding, slightly embarrassed that it had been Zach's. Panting, I tried to sit up but was pushed back down.

"Sit back for a minute. I've got to fix up your father." Tanner had already gotten to work, stripping off Cole's shirt so that I could see the wound. It was shallow enough, his arm was in much worse shape though it looked to be better than mine had been. I was relieved, and dragged Mads down to my level so I could check her back. Chunks of her fur had been ripped out, but as shaken up as she was nothing seemed super deep. I sat up, ignoring Tanner's previous warnings and motioned for Zach to hold her down while I cleaned her up a bit. The poor girl just let there and let me do it, though her eyes never left mine and I felt terrible. Whether or not she knew I was helping her, I still tried to quickly finish what I was doing so that the stinging would subside. We didn't really have bandages that would stick because of her remaining fur, so we bunched up a few nearby pairs of boxers to stop the blood and wrapped around her body with gauze to keep it in place. "You're gonna be alright girly." I whispered into her ear, ruffling the top of her head gently. I still felt winded, the majority of the animal had landed on my stomach when I fired, and I definitely felt disgustingly sticky with blood. "Now I have to grab more things." I felt bad that I had managed to screw up our cache already.

"It's fine, I'll grab you another shirt. Sit tight." Zach placed a hand on my shoulder, hoisting himself up and wandering within my eyesight. I reached out for my bat, remembering the vibrations as they had raced up my hand. So similar to when I had hit that man in the gift shop. I was glad that Zach stayed nearby, and Mads remained sitting beside my injured leg as I slid the bat back into my backpack, trying to shoulder it onto my back. It took a bit of wiggling, every time I jostled my leg the searing pain raced up my thigh but I eventually managed to get it up and on my shoulders. I didn't know how I was going to get home like this, it would take some limping for sure.

Zach returned, carefully folding up a shirt into my bag and zipping it back up. He slid it off of my shoulders, completely against my protesting, and slipped it up onto his own. "We're not going to put more weight on you stupid, not when you won't even be able to support your own." I shut up and fumed, glaring at him in between winces. "Just do what we say, we can't bring you home broken and mangled to Trent. Besides, you've gotta heal up so we can worry about Mads." Okay fine, I would give him that. I was already worrying over her, there would be no way to stop her from biting at the bandages and slowing down her healing. I knew they would keep me in the house for as long as possible, hell my father would use this as a perfect example for why I shouldn't be allowed out to begin with, but at least I could force her into bed rest with me.

"Fine." I hissed, hating being incapacitated like this. "I can't believe this though, what the hell is a lion doing in here?" I nudged it with my undestroyed leg, before recoiling in horror. I couldn't help that my hands went to cover my mouth, and I nearly cried on the spot.

"Oh my god, I killed it." I had killed something, I was a murderer. "What have I done."

Zach seemed surprised, as if he hadn't noticed my terrible atrocities against Mother Nature. Typical boy. "You can't think of it that way. It was going to kill us. It swiped at your father! It would have eaten one of us as soon as it got a chance." I peeked at it from behind my hands. The poor thing did look decidedly skinny. "I guess whatever managed to get out of the zoo had to find food the old fashioned way. So stop feeling bad about yourself." He grabbed my wrists, making me look him in the eye. "You saved us all, and did exactly what we all would have done. You're not a terrible person. Sure it sucks, but this isn't a Disney movie. It's pretty unlikely that you could have sung at it and made your own lion army to ride into battle with."

"I can't sing." I huffed, though he had made me feel a little bit better. It was us against it, and I had a little lion cub of my own to get back to. "Help me up?" Zach regarded my request for a second, before lifting himself and taking my offered arm. He hoisted me up, ignoring my intake of breath as I hissed. My leg wouldn't support the weight, and buckled instantly. Ignoring his 'I told you so' look, I let him lift my arm over his shoulder, leaning into him so he could help me walk. "This is going to be impossible."

"But you're going to be alright, and that's all that matters." Cole spoke up. Tanner had bandaged his arm into a sling and aside from the paleness of his skin he seemed in better shape than I was. "You're both okay, right Madigan?" He patted Mads on the head when she shuffled over, taking note of our handiwork with a smile. "I'm pretty sure that we've had enough excitement for one day. We should head back to the house." Nobody was in any shape to ward off another attack, and didn't lions hunt in packs or prides or whatever terrifying group they travelled in?

It was slow going. Every patch of rough terrain made me cry out under my breath. Zach did his best, but there was no way he could make the trip gentler on my weary bones. I ignored his sideways glances as best I could, Mads leash wrapped around my hand. It was fairly unnecessary, she wasn't going to let me out of her sight again for what was possibly the next three days. "Nobody would ever believe this." Not that I knew the status of very many people I would relay the story to. For all I knew they were all dead. I tried not to dwell on that depressing thought, only focusing on the blurry outline as the house came into view. I was thankful for it, as I couldn't take very much more walking. Not that I would ever admit it to the men, especially not since they had made a point of checking up on me every five minutes.

What had taken us on a little while in the morning ended up being two hours, my leg only impeding our speed. By the time we got past the gate and up the winding gravelled drive I was about ready to drop, and Zach was carrying more than his fair share of weight as we crossed through the door. Miranda called out a hello, and I dropped Mads leash, letting her drag it behind her throughout the house. I heard Trent greet her, and I hoped he wouldn't prod at her bandages. Miranda must have spotted her, as she came out into view with a worried look on her face. "What the hell happened?" She grabbed my backpack off of Zach's shoulder, letting him settle me onto the couch. Trent and Mads rounded the corner, with a worried expression on his tiny face. To be honest, on him it was almost laughable. It perked me up seeing him, and I held my arms out to the little twerp. Zach lifted him up onto the couch with me, and to my surprise Trent made sure to gingerly avoid the leg I had propped up on the cushions.

"Are you okay?" He grabbed my face in both of his tiny hands, turning it to inspect both sides. His fingers were warm, and I smiled into his palms. "Of course we're okay. We only had to fight a lion!"

His eyes widened and his mouth dropped open in a gasp. "Are you for real?" I nodded, patting my leg as evidence. Cole passed me the bag, and I rummaged through it for what I had managed to get him. "I hope you were busy making us a few drawings, cause I have some more for you to do." I handed over the colouring book and crayons, and he whooped and leapt off the couch with them.

"I made up a few riddles to keep him occupied today." Miranda spoke up from her spot on the chair, glancing at Tanner to make sure he was unmarked. "He was brilliant though, we even had a bit of a nap." She worried at her lip, looking upset for a moment. "He has nightmares, so we had to cut that a bit short." I had expected that. There was no way you stayed in an apartment with your rotting mother's corpse for god knew how many days completely alone. No eight year old should ever have to go through that.

"He's a tough little cookie, he'll get over it." I looked over the colourings he brought me. Kid was pretty good; he would probably have a blast with what I had brought him. "I hope." Child rearing was hard, I never knew if what I was doing was right and I had only had the little whelp for a day and a half. How my parents had done it for eighteen years was completely beyond me. Miranda nodded in what I assumed she hoped to be a reassuring way, and moved back to the kitchen to continue cooking. My lunch seemed hours away, and it was probably a good thing that my appetite had returned. I couldn't be dying if I was hungry.

"You handled yourself well out there." Tanner was leaning up against the doorframe, watching Miranda as she puttered around the kitchen. "One of us would be dead if it wasn't for your quick shooting." He turned and left the room and I was left stunned, his compliment completely unexpected. Zach shook his head, gingerly lifting my leg and setting my foot in his lap so that he could sit on the couch as well. This to me was more surprising than a lion attack, though I couldn't say that I didn't enjoy it.

"I never want to do any of this ever again." I suddenly slumped back into the cushion, all energy that I had put out for Trent to prove that I was okay completely draining from my body. "This sucks." I would be off my feet for a few days, and probably going crazy at home while the three of them risked their lives out there. "We need to get a car or a van or something." The roads were clear enough, and we had passed by a gas station. There was no reason that we should have to walk everywhere, giant earthquake caused cracks in the cement aside. "I want a motorcycle."

"I don't think any of us are going to let that happen." Zach laughed, leaning himself back into the couch. "Your dad didn't even want to let you come, I doubt he's going to let you ride on a motorcycle." He had a point, and I had no energy to argue. So much for saving all of them and commanding their respect.

Everyone slowly drifted back into the room with bowls of soup, and Zach set my leg back on the couch to grab ours. I heard him call Trent into the kitchen, and the boy came back in with his bowl, carefully taking steps with his eyes on the liquid so he didn't spill it. He settled against my leg, sitting on the floor with wide eyes on Tanner when he re-entered. I ruffled his hair and gave his shoulder an affectionate squeeze, hoping to let him know that nothing was going to happen. If anything I had proven today that I sure as hell had a say in what went on back home.

Miranda began peppering us with questions as we ate and I sat back, letting Tanner and my dad fill her in. She gaped at me when they told her how I had killed the lioness, as if unbelieving that I was capable of such a feat. "You shot it?" I glared at her, I had been planning on keeping Trent in the dark about that little detail but now the cat was out of the bag and bleeding on the floor back at the mall. Using the opportunity of a mouth full of soup, I nodded and motioned for Cole to continue speaking. She let them finish with few questions, excusing herself to collect the bowls and wash up so none of us had to do anything. I wondered if she felt as guilty as I would if our roles had been switched, staying at home and babysitting while the rest of us went out and risked our lives for answers. Not that anyone had expected anything of that calibre when we set out today. If we had, there was no chance that Cole would have even let me take a step out of the door.

Trent brought me some paper and the crayons once we were finished, sitting beside me on the couch and narrating while I drew. He was full of ideas and we filled several pages with his nonsensical stories. It was relaxing for me, letting my mind let go of everything that had happened in the past week, and I wondered if it was the same for him. "I have another surprise for you." I leaned down to ruffle through the bag, coming up with the stuffed dog I had snagged on our expedition. He took it and hugged it to his chest, immediately leaping down to show Mads and dance it along the floor beside her. "It's your boyfriend Madigan! Woof woof woof!" He barked and snuffled the dog's nose to her own. She gently bit at its head, but it only took one note of admonishment from me for her to let go. "That's not how you give kisses Madigan!" He chastised her, pulling lightly on one ear. She harrumphed and laid down on her side, sighing as if she had the most difficult job in the world.

The rest of the night passed in quiet amiability, with no more surprises or harsh words. Tanner seemed to have taken my words to heart and wasn't going to push the Trent issue for now at least and I was grateful. I had little to no energy and I had to count on what I had to get me into bed at the end of the night. Zach and Trent were settled on the floor, the former attempting to teach the latter the finer points of chess. Trent was trying, but I could tell he was getting bored and was soon galloping the knight around the room while making horse noises. "Let me have that." I held out my hand and he dropped it in my palm obediently, going back to the dog he had named Bob and galloping him around instead. "I'll play you."

Zach settled the board into my lap, waving away all of my admittances that I was terrible at the game. We played for a while, and the game took all of my concentration. He was fantastic, and quickly beat me twice before I gave up and passed the board to my father. Zach destroyed him too, only losing to Tanner in an admirable struggle for dominance. It was then that I realized how late it was, the sun had dipped underneath the horizon a while ago. "Time for bed whelp." I called out to Trent, and it took a few more tries before he was actually ready to go upstairs. "Zach's gonna tuck you in tonight, I don't think I can get back down the stairs once I'm up there and he tells really good stories." Zach sighed and swung the boy over his shoulder, ignoring the squiggling child who laughed and squirmed for escape. I hugged him goodnight and sent them on their way, Zach making train noises all the way up the stairs.

As soon as they were out of hearing I turned to Cole. "As soon as I can walk again I'm going back out. Don't use this as an excuse to coop me up in here." I could already see that he was ready to disagree with me. "Tanner said it himself, one of us would have been dead without me and I know it." Cole glared at Tanner, who threw his hands up in defense and tried to bring the attention back to me. "I did say it, but only because it's true."

Cole sighed and rubbed his temples, I knew I was getting to him. "It's too dangerous out there. We got lucky, there was only one of them next time. But most things hunt in packs, I can't chance you getting hurt like this again." Like I was the only one who had gotten hurt in this little expedition. "Try to keep me home and I'll just sneak out and follow you. Then I won't even be nearby for you to keep an eye on." My remark got a glare, and I knew I had gone a bit too far with my comments.

"With all due respect sir, we could use her out there. If it hadn't been for Alice..." Zach trailed off, frozen on the stairs by Cole's icy gaze. "Well if it hadn't been for her we might not all have made it back." He was definitely not winning any brownie points with my father but it was nice of him to try anyways. Cole creased his brow but seemed to give up, muttering some kind of acquiescence under his breath before stalking away like an angry teenager. I considered it a small victory and let out a breath, slumping against the couch.

"That's enough excitement for one day." Tanner nudged Miranda, shepherding her up to their room. She had been dozing off in her chair since we had begun talking, either bored with the conversation or due to her night medication kicking in. I was fighting the urge for sleep too, and Zach helped me back up the stairs. I hoped that I could smooth things over with Cole in the morning, but I knew he would eventually get over it just like he had with many things in the past. "Thanks for that." I whispered as he set me down on the bed. I was mindful not to wake Trent who was curled up sound asleep like a tiny cat. "He thinks of me as a child still I think." Zach shrugged away my thanks, rummaging through my things to toss me my pyjamas and spare me the act of bending over to get them.

"It was no problem, I figured you needed some help." He grinned, standing up and mussing with the back of his hair. "Uh, speaking of help…" He trailed off, looking pointedly at my leg. It took a few moments before I could stop being uncomfortable with his gaze on my legs and realize what he was implying. "Oh uh, no I'm okay." They had cut off everything at my thigh so they could bandage it properly. The bottom half had been shredded anyways. "I think I can slide this over. Besides, you're already not in my dad's good books. No sense in adding to that by taking off my pants." I swore I could hear him heave a sigh of relief and he gave me a quick peck on the top of my head before leaving and gently closing the door behind him. I was left stunned on the bed sheets and it took a few seconds before I could gather my errant thoughts to myself and begin attempting to undress myself.

Four minutes of struggling later and I was down to just my jeans and quietly swearing under my breath.

I had needed him.

Day 7

The calendar on the wall that someone had begun to thoughtfully mark off with X's so we could keep track of the date said it had been seven days. I swore and rubbed the back of my neck. How the hell had it been a week and we were no closer than when we had started?

Dressing this morning had been a bit of a challenge, as my leg was stiff and covered in bruises. Trent had been kind enough to fetch my dad who was tasked with the embarrassing job of dressing his adult daughter. I sent him away when my pants were on, ignoring the awkward glances and pulling the t-shirt over my head. Standing was still incredibly difficult, my leg couldn't support much weight before it buckled, and I had to rely on people to get me up and down the stairs as well as from room to room when there wasn't something to hold my body up with. I couldn't even scootch down the stairs like someone with a broken leg, so even that dignity had been stripped from me. I wasn't looking forward to my first shower.

Everyone was already seated in the kitchen when Cole helped me limp into a chair. Miranda slid a plate in front of me, and I cursed her ability to still do things while diving into my delicious looking plate of eggs.

"First order of business," Cole spoke over my voracious eating, and I poured a glass of juice for Trent who looked as bright eyed and bushy tailed as always. "We're going back out there. We've got to get some actual weapons, with only one gun it's going to be impossible to fend things off if they come at us in larger groups than two. If we can find anything we will be having target practice so I can tell that nobody is going to accidentally shoot anyone in the back of the head." He looked directly at me when he said that but I waved him off, having been through the rounds of training and gun safety a million times. I doubted how likely he was to find some actual guns, but it felt like a safe thing to have. Hopefully he ignored his desire to view me as a child and made sure I got one. I was a pretty damn good shot, had taken airgun classes in summer camp and been the top of my group.

I was dreading them leaving knowing that it would mean me being left alone with Miranda for an entire day. Zach wasn't receiving my telepathy telling him to eat slower, and I cursed him for being close-minded. They had also decided to leave Mads behind to heal a bit more. We had peeked under her bandages and they hadn't looked any worse, but there was no sense in sending her out there to tear open a scab. Still, it was going to be a long boring day of child rearing and I wasn't looking forward to it in the least.

"We'll try to bring you back some crutches." Zach leaned against the doorframe in the entryway once everyone had finished. I fidgeted in my position on the stairs, uncomfortable even with sitting. "I'm hoping that by the time you get back I won't need them." I scowled down at my injury, cursing it for the thousandth time that morning. For now I had a stick that someone had found in the back yard, painfully whittled down to help me hobble around. The thing was super uncomfortable and I already hated it, but it helped. "Well, you rest up and work on healing then champ."

Curse him, why did he have to smile like that? "And you work on coming home safe." I muttered, biting back on the words but it was too late. "I don't want to lose you to some murdering lioness. Any of you." I attempted to backpedal on the last bit, turning to look at my dad in an attempt to throw everyone off of the scent. Not that anyone was paying any attention to the mini drama that was unfolding in my mind.

"Who's going to carry you up the stairs if we don't come back." Zach laughed and awkwardly patted me on the head, shouldering his bag and turning to look at Trent while he walked out of the door. "Be good and I'll bring back a board game or something." Cards would be nice. We hadn't managed to find a deck in this whole place and it would have been cool to even play solitaire while I moped the hours away until they came home. How the hell had Miranda done it yesterday?

The door shut and they were gone, leaving us all self-consciously milling in the foyer. "Can I take Mads outside for a walk?" Trent asked, tugging at my sleeve and dropping the leash at my feet. I didn't really see a problem with it, the backyard was fenced in and I could watch him from the kitchen table. "Okay, but only for a little while. She needs to rest too." I hefted myself up, noticing that Miranda had made herself scarce. It took a few painful minutes of hopping to get into the kitchen, but I had myself seated back at the table and he dropped off the pad of paper and crayons for me to play with. "I'll call you when it's time to come in. Be gentle."

The cool air whooshed in through the door when he slid it open, Mads trotting along with him outside. It would be getting cold soon, we would need to prepare for that. What were we going to eat if we were out here for much longer? The garden was already producing its last fruits and veggies of the season. I supposed that we could freeze a bunch to last us, but it would be a lot of dry, tasteless cans of whatever we could find from here on out. I huffed and went to make myself a tea, grateful for the counters to lean on.

As the pot had finished boiling Miranda wandered in, turning down my offer for a mug. I quietly finished brewing it, and was mixing in my sugar before she spoke. "He looks like he's settling in." She was leaned up against the sliding glass door, watching Trent and Mads chase each other around the yard. "Yeah, I'm glad. I was a bit worried, I still am." I shrugged, bringing the mug with me back to the table so I could drink without worrying about balancing.

"I was just wondering. I don't know very much about you Alice. I know the basics, your dad spoke of you a lot before we found you. He said you were off to college in the fall. For art?" I nodded, surprised that she was perpetuating a conversation. Miranda hadn't wanted anything to do with me since day one. "But he didn't mention anything about Zach. He's your boyfriend?" The question caught me off guard, but I managed to give her a short no before turning back to my tea. What was she prying in that for? "Oh, I had just assumed. You two seem very close." She sat with me, and to be honest it made me slightly uncomfortable. I didn't exactly see this as her stretching out the proverbial olive branch of friendship.

"What about you Miranda?" The words were out of my mouth before I realized that it could be a touchy subject, she had come here straight from a car accident. "Sorry. Um, if you don't want to talk about it that's alright." But she waved my apologies away and began telling me about how she had been driving along the highway when someone spun out of control and t-boned her, throwing her from the car and breaking her arm. How Tanner and my father had found her in the hospital, one living person among many corpses. How they had lived in a torn up tent for a day, how he had never slept and was constantly trying to push them to get out and search. How they had found this place, and Tanner had jimmied the wires to give them access. I learned about her past, that she had been a marine biology student and was visiting the city for a vacation. How she hadn't been able to get in contact with her family and was worried sick. She was alone in a strange city and it was going to hell.

At one point I thought she might start to cry, and I was unprepared for it. It was relieving that she didn't, but the silence made me stand and call Trent in from his playing. "Do you mind watching him for a bit? I'm dying for a shower and I feel like it's going to take a while." I gestured at my leg, knowing that I was going to have to peel the bandages off and wash it out. She agreed and I left Trent with my doodles and an apple for a snack. Mads followed me up the stairs, worrying at my ankles and nearly causing me to fall up them twice.

The bathroom door shut and I leaned up against it, sighing at my escape from everyone for once. I began the laborious task of undressing and was on the edge of the tub contemplating the bandage. It would probably hurt to remove, and was guaranteed to be pretty gnarly. Mads regarded me from her place on the floor, and I imagined that she understood and shared in my pain. I took a deep breath and let it out in a hiss as I unravelled the gauze from my leg. My thigh was mottled with purple bruises, but the actual cut itself looked okay. I edged myself down into the bath I had made, stifling a screech when the hot water hit the wound. I let myself soak for what felt like ages, not even bothering to move until the water grew cold. Mads had taken to hanging her head over the edge of the tub and biting at whatever ripples my body made in the water, and had to be pushed out of the way with one pruney hand when I decided to get out. It felt nice to be clean again, all of the sweat and blood washed out of my hair and my skin pink and wrinkled.

I limped out of the bathroom, startled to see Trent quietly playing in the room. He covered his eyes while I dressed, telling me that Miranda had asked him to play in here so she could have some quiet time. I understood, her medicine sometimes gave her aggravated headaches and made her pretty tired, but Trent was a quiet enough kid to begin with and I doubted that he had been making that much noise. Leaving him to his colouring I hobbled down the stairs, banging my stick against the railing and nearly catapulting myself down them. I would be happy when I could walk on two feet instead of three again.

Miranda was in the living room when I got down there, peering over the back of the couch in a typical model pose. She looked deep in thought, her reflection in the window showed just how distracted she was. She didn't even notice I was in the room until I knocked on the frame and spooked her. "Sorry, just wanted to reprieve you of your duty. Did he give you trouble or something?" She shook her head, explaining that she had had a migraine and needed the quiet. I didn't push, but left to explore the remaining rooms that I hadn't seen yet.

Mads was acting odd, spending an inordinate amount of time sniffing around the room. I chalked it up to her being antsy to go outside and ignored it until I could drag myself back to the kitchen door. Instead I walked amongst the rooms, touching things and rearranging them, trying to create a story of whoever had lived here. I hoped that they were just away on vacation, and hadn't seen what this city had become. That they were somewhere safe and were with whoever they loved. I thought of Zach, how I wished that he would have been far away on one of those family outings his parents always loved and he begrudgingly attended.

I wanted to be useful, so I combed through a few bookshelves looking for anything that Trent might be able to use. I was hoping for math, or even a child friendly storybook, but I was pretty let down and returned to the stairs with my meagre pile of books. Mads took off like a rocket, barking her head off but it was too early for everyone to be home. "Hush you maniacal milliner." I tossed her outside, watching as she romped confusedly around the perimeter of the backyard still barking. I half wished she would shut up, worried she would draw more beasties to us, but was also half relieved to see her enjoying herself like a dog should.

The rest of the afternoon passed at a slow crawl and I barely made it through the day. Trent was content to read through some of the easier books I had found for him and impressed both Miranda and I with his spectacular literary aptitude. I doodled on every surface I could get my hands on, and Miranda mostly napped on and off. When I was sure that my wits would break Mads announced the arrival of our boys, circling the front door and yapping excitedly. She pounced on them when they came in the door, and I made my way as quickly as I could to greet them as well.

Nobody seemed to be in terrible shape and I let out a sigh of relief. "No exciting things today?" I asked, checking them over once more for any signs of blood. They were quiet, hopefully just due to exhaustion, but let me know that no they hadn't seen anything. Dinner was just the reheated soup, so we had a fair bit of time on our hands before anyone had anything serious to do.

"I brought some stuff back for Trent." Zach told me, dumping his backpack on my bedspread. Games, cards and even a candy bar tumbled out and onto the sheet. I immediately hid the chocolate, wanting to save that for a special occasion until we could grab more. "The games are perfect, thanks." I sat on the bed, rifling through them to sort out stuff for him to do tomorrow. A sketchbook snagged on something else and fell to the floor. "What's that for?" It was empty, I realized as I bent down to pick it up. "He likes to draw but I don't think he needs the heavier paper to do it."

Zach seemed embarrassed, handing me a set of pencils as well. "Those are kind of for you. I didn't want to come home without anything for you too." I was touched by the gesture, and it was a little funny watching him squirm with embarrassment. It was so often me in that position. "Thanks, it'll be nice not to have to draw in crayon for a while." I grinned, probably a little too wide, and tried to hide the blush I could feel forming somewhere around my cheekbones. "Help me downstairs? I should probably help them divvy up the rest of the loot." It was no secret that Cole had brought home some weaponry from their stop at the precinct. As much as I had hoped for something badass like a bow and arrow I also hoped for something I could actually master in very little time. Knowing how graceless I was, something I didn't have to do more than aim was probably my best bet.

When we joined the rest of them I could see that Cole was already starting Trent on the cursory gun talk. It involved fun topics such as: only pointing the gun at something you wanted dead, never pointing it at yourself, and never pointing it period unless you were in grave danger. I remembered the whole spiel from a million years ago, could practically recite it along with him. Still, the part where he took the pistol apart and explained all of its bits and pieces was still pretty cool.

"Guns off of the dinner table." Miranda seemed a bit edgy, skirting the table and keeping her distance from the weapons as she carried a fistful of silverware. Tanner followed behind her with the pot of soup, and we all helped ourselves once Cole has cleared his toys from the table. The conversation flowed a bit easier now, we had all gotten used to one another and for a moment I saw us as a rather dysfunctional family. An extremely dysfunctional family, as I realized that Trent was still moderately terrified of Tanner, my father treated Zach as cool as ever and Miranda barely spoke to me. No sign of the sob story she had told me earlier, and how she had "confessed" that she was "just so excited to have another girl around to combat all of this testosterone!".

When everything was all cleaned up Cole announced that nobody would be scavenging tomorrow, instead we would be practicing our marksmanship with the air rifles he had managed to scoop from the camping section of a department store. It made more sense, that way we would get a feel for it without wasting whatever ammo he had managed to commandeer in their previous trip. And it lightened the mood considerably.

With nobody worrying about what tomorrow would hold for us outside of our gates, everyone was much more relaxed and willing to hang out. A few rounds of crazy eights happened, with Tanner only joining in when we turned it into a poker tournament. I was hopeless, only winning a few rounds due to sheer dumb luck. I had about as much idea about how the game went as Trent did, and the two of us peeked at each others cards and tried to remember what all of the hands were. Eventually we played as an unofficial team and still managed to barely win a few hands. We played until Trent's eyes got droopy and he began to nod off into my lap, and Zach scooped him up to put in bed. I followed them upstairs, tucking him in with the stuffed Bob and making sure he could still see a crack of light under the door. Mads jumped up onto the bed, curling up beside him in my spot and huffing, watching as I went to close the door.

I leaned against the doorframe for a moment with Zach, unsure of what to do next. I was too wired to sleep, but definitely not in any shape to do anything even remotely adventurous. "I maybe kind of found a portable DVD player and some movies." He shrugged like it wasn't a big deal, but we both knew it was. A movie would be the closest thing to normalcy we had experienced in nearly a week. Hell, the only reason we all ate together was to try and piece together a little of what we had all had once. "If you wanted to watch something?" I desperately wanted to watch something, but I managed to hold it together as we asked around.

Nobody shared in our desire to zone out to a screen and we were left to our own devices in the living room. Zach turned down the lights while I settled in on the couch, trying to find the most comfortable position on the L shaped cushions. We had agreed on some horror movie that neither of us had seen, which was surprising considering our group of friends had powered through several of them one summer. I freaked out easily, but I needed something to get my mind off of everything that had happened, and Zach probably had it worse.

During the course of the movie I found myself panicking and sliding closer to him unintentionally, a stance I would then correct as subtly as I could. On my fifth time of covering my eyes when the music got too intense he tapped my shoulder – when had he stretched his arm along the back of the couch? – and pulled me in towards him. This was easier for me, as I could now burrow my face into his shoulder to close my eyes as well as cover my ears when things started to remind me of that encounter only days ago in the hotel.

I reminded myself that this was just a movie, and I had managed to survive my experience much better than these dimwitted blonde girls. The movie ended in a stereotypically cheesy way, and we were left sitting in the dark while the hushed sounds of the house closed in around us. I involuntarily shuddered, grabbing at the blanket that had previously only covered my outstretched leg and pulled it up around my waist. Apparently the adults had also gone to bed, with Cole nowhere to be found as we were currently sitting on his. He had probably taken up residence in the office or something to let us keep watching which was pretty cool of him I would admit.

It seemed like a lifetime before either of us broke the silence, and I was content to just sit here forever just listening to the sounds of the house creaking and Mads pacing around the room upstairs. "Miranda came into my room last night." He whispered into my ear, the hairs on the back of my neck rising in response. My temper rose as well.

"What the hell? Creepy. What did she want?" I tried to keep my tone even and uninterested, even if I was dying on the inside.

"She said just to check up on me, that she couldn't sleep and was worried. She woke me up but came in and sat on the bed and talked or whatever."

He fidgeted with the hem of the blanket, anxiously twisting the braids between his thumb and forefinger. "I was kind of uncomfortable to be honest. She kept putting her hand on my leg." This didn't surprise me, I had expected something of the sort from the start. "I thought that her and Tanner were together?"

"They've only known each other for a few days, he's useful to her and she's pretty enough." The venom in my voice was mild enough that he didn't seem to detect it. "Plus he seems to know what he's doing with that medicine." The rest of us could only guess at what her mending bones would need to properly heal.

"She's not that pretty, but I guess she's the only one around he's got a chance with." I barely heard the second part of his sentence, as my heart was throwing up butterflies into my stomach. "She asked me a lot about you actually. Like her bringing you up was going to make me more comfortable." I wanted to suggest that he bunk with us, but the logical solution would be for him to lock his door so I pointed that out and he agreed. We settled back into silence, my mind roving through all the ways I could kill Miranda and not have the blame pinned on me.

"I want to visit my dad soon." He mentioned quietly, jogging me from all of my murderous plotting and I immediately felt guilty again. I didn't know what to say and I pulled the blanket over him as well. "I'm sure we can do it. Or if you don't want to tell anyone we could just go. Or I could cover for you and you could go alone, but I don't like the idea of some roaming landbeast tearing you to shreds." By the time I was ready to be up and walking who knew how hungry those things would be. I could feel him nod against me, though I wasn't sure exactly what he was agreeing to.

The light flashed on and we jumped apart, startled into our own ends of the couch. Miranda stood there, holding an empty glass and looking utterly confused. "I want some water." She murmured, obviously not understanding why we hadn't miraculously turned into kitchen sinks for her. I wanted to destroy her like she had destroyed my peaceful half sleeping, but I remained on the couch while Zach fetched her some water and listened to whatever whispered rambling she was subjecting him to. I didn't see her again, assuming that she had gone back upstairs to bed. Zach didn't return to the couch, instead wordlessly helping me to my feet and up the stairs. When I tried to ask him what had happened he just shook his head and got me up to my door.

"Hey." I whispered, grabbing his wrist before he could turn and say goodnight. "Are you alright?" I was worried by the look on his face, a cross almost between disgust and awkwardness. She must have said something to wind him up like this, but I didn't know what.

"Yeah. She's just drunk and doesn't know what the hell she's talking about." He half snapped, turning to look at her closed door as he spoke. I shushed him, as with every word his voice got a little bit louder until it was almost normal speaking volume. "Drunk girls are the worst Alice." He grinned, his face melding back into what I was used to seeing, and tucked a strand of hair behind my ear. I didn't take offense by his words, knowing that I was absolutely the worst whenever I had snuck off with friends to imbibe. It was nice to know that I wasn't the only one who couldn't handle her liquor.

"Some of us aren't that bad." I lied, wobbling a bit on my makeshift crutch. They hadn't managed to find anything for me to balance better on, but I would hopefully be back on my feet tomorrow. Even if I was just well enough to scoot around the house I would be pretty happy, and putting on my pants by myself in the morning would be awesome. "But you should get to bed. You've had a long day and I don't want to keep you up any longer." He seemed like he wanted to stay up and unwind for a bit longer, but that could obviously just be me putting my wishes on him and seeing things that didn't exist. I tended to do that a lot. "Unless you want more company?"

He shook his head no, reaching behind me to open my door. "Get yourself to bed, you don't want to put more strain on your leg by standing around on it." He shooed me inside, ever mindful not to wake the sleeping child who was nestled quietly underneath the pile of blankets, and grabbed my pyjamas from the messy pile I had left them in on the floor. I sighed and sat lightly on the edge of the bed, fiddling with the drawstring of my pants. Now that I was re-bandaged and cleaned up, my leg wasn't nearly as stiff and the cotton track pants wouldn't be that hard to shimmy over the gauze. "Goodnight Alice, let me know if you need anything." He ruffled my hair while I was left hoping for another tiny goodnight kiss and turned to leave.

"Zach." I called out softly, stopping him at the door. "I was serious about visiting your dad. We'll figure something out. If you want to talk about it, you know where to find me." I finished lamely, shrugging to let him know that it was no problem. I still didn't know how to approach the subject of his father's death, and still grappled daily with how unfair it was that I had made it out of everything relatively unscathed. "Goodnight." He nodded at me and left, leaving me to drop my body onto the bed and groan. Trent had become quite the sound sleeper now that he had his first taste of stability in god knew how long, and I was grateful for that. I patted the bed sheet as an invitation for Mads while I undressed, and she settled herself down on the blankets with a hefty sigh. She was as antsy as I was to go back out there, though she was closer to being ready than I was.

"Tomorrow we give her hangover hell." I whispered to the dog, playing with her ears. "We will be so loud she won't know what hit her." Sure it was pretty immature of me, but all was fair in love and destroying your enemies.

Or something like that.

Day 8

Trent was up and out of bed before I even managed to pry apart my eyelids. Mads was also nowhere to be seen, but I imagined that someone had either let her out or she was simply meandering around the house waiting for me to get up. The upper floor was quiet, and I contemplated how early it was while I changed. I wasn't used to this whole getting up with the sun thing, as it was quite the departure from what I had gone through all summer, but it was probably for the best. There were more hours in the day to scavenge with, a task that nobody felt comfortable with at night.

Yawning, I pulled a new shirt over my head. There was no sense in going through the misery of changing my pyjama pants until I was ready to shower anyways. I made the bed quickly and stepped back to admire my handiwork for a moment before locating my crutch. I contemplated it for a moment, unsure if I could stand under my own power today and took a few wobbly steps. My leg flared up with each step, but it was no longer the unbearable pressure that I was used to the last few days. I rolled up my pant leg to see if I was bleeding again and was satisfied to find out that no, I wasn't. Today could potentially be a good day.

By the time I got down the stairs I was still okay, though the jarring pressure from going downstairs had definitely brought a small tear to my eye. Baby steps were going to be necessary and it sucked that patience wasn't one of my virtues. Cole was up, drinking a coffee out of a ceramic mug and watching Mads as she romped through the yard. Tanner, Miranda and Zach were nowhere to be seen, though the sounds of some kids movie in the next room lent me a clue as to where Trent could be found. I muttered a greeting and helped myself to the stack of toast and remaining eggs off of my father's plate, not exactly feeling up to standing up at the stove and cooking something on my own feet.

"You're up and about, let me see." Cole patted his thigh and I obediently placed my leg on it, watching curiously as he rolled up my pant leg to see what was what. He tapped at the edge of the bandage and I managed to keep a straight face through the pain, which caused him to grin. He either knew I was faking it or was just happy to see that my leg hadn't fallen off from blood poisoning or something. "Well it looks like you're doing a lot better. Probably going to be all healed up before I am." He gently let my leg down and I placed my bare foot against the cool ceramic tiles.

"That's what I'm hoping for." I shoved a piece of toast in my mouth, suddenly voraciously hungry now that I had passed inspection. "How soon before I can get back out there?" I didn't enjoy seeing his smile turn into a hard little line, but I was going to broach the subject sooner or later. "I mean, I know I've probably got another day here but maybe tomorrow?"

"Maybe tomorrow. We'll see." He tersely agreed and I let the subject drop, knowing I could use this day to practice my aim would mean that it wasn't a total waste of a day. "You just keep focused on getting mended and let me worry about your curfew." I nodded, happy to placate him. I knew that I would eventually just undermine his decision but it was best to let him live in his ignorance for now. There was no harm in him knowing I was safe for a few days before I completely destroyed that.

"Has Trent eaten yet? Trent! Come here you little tadpole!" I called out, not mindful at all about my volume and those who were sleeping above me. I heard him pause the movie and come skipping into the kitchen. I told him to grab his bowl while I located the cereal, pouring him a glass of juice that he all but poured down his throat in his haste to get back to whatever movie he was watching. "Zach managed to find you some kiddie shows huh?" I asked, starting in on my eggs while he nodded with his mouth full of cheerio's. "That's pretty neat." My need for conversation in the morning spent, the three of us settled into a comfortable silence broken only by Cole getting up to let Mads in from outside. I patted her cold fur, pushing her nose away from the table when she sniffed at it.

"Puppy food for the doggy." I led her to the pantry and scooped her a few cups of kibble, which she downed with as much energy as Trent had. When I turned back around he was gone and I heard the distant tinny sounds of the show being restarted. "Feh, kids." I caught the smile on Cole's face and laughed. "Bet you had hoped I'd never be a teenage mom huh?" He tossed a soggy cheerio at me in response.

Zach was the next to come down, all bed headed and sleepy and adorable. He yawned a greeting, settling into the table with a cup of juice and nothing else. We chit chatted for a bit, though it was mostly me speaking. It was clear that Cole didn't exactly like my friend, though I couldn't imagine why. I pushed them on the topic of strategies for today and that got them talking well enough. Sitting back to admire my handiwork, I almost didn't notice it when Miranda skulked in. Almost.

"Morning Miranda!" I chirped at a slightly higher volume than usual, holding back a smirk when I saw her wince slightly. "How are you feeling today?" I didn't even mind that she only growled her reply. Not if I could maker her suffer in even the slightest, pettiest way. "We were just talking about what they should look for when they get back out there." I rambled on, ignoring the odd looks from both men and continuing to talk with a forced sounding happiness. "I'm pretty excited to start target practice today though! Aren't you?"

"Sure." She all but slammed her coffee down at the table, a sound that made her drop her head into her hands. I smirked down at my now empty plate of eggs and revelled in the destruction of my enemy.

Cole excused himself to wander into the living room. I knew he had a soft spot for Trent and also for whatever weird cartoons Zach had managed to score. I was grateful to not have to explain myself, though I knew I was going to get a talking to as soon as we were alone in a room together. I made a mental note not to be alone with my father until he would have forgotten all about this. It wasn't exactly something he would either understand or appreciate.

I could see Zach trying to catch my eye but I knew that he would quickly figure out what I was up to if I so much as looked at him. I tended to wear how guilty I was directly on my sleeve. I laid off a bit, knowing that I would have to spend the entire day with her and was unwilling to be the subject of a murder, and quietly played with the remnants of the crumbs on my plate. Even the sound of fork scratching against ceramic seemed to prove too much for the blonde beauty to handle, and she stormed off with her coffee cup in hand. I chalked it up as a victory that was long overdue, and only then did I look up to meet Zach's knowing gaze.

"What was that all about?" He asked, and in response I gave him my most innocent shrug. He wasn't going to let me get away with it apparently, pushing aside my reply about her maybe not being a morning person. "Come off it Alice, we both know what you were doing. I guess a better question would have been why."

I didn't want to give him the real answer for that, so I settled with what I hoped would be the most plausible. "I just wanted to give her a taste of her own medicine. I'm sorry." I wasn't really, but it would be nice if he didn't think I was a completely terrible person for now at least. "I didn't think I'd make her run. I really should have rethought this, she's going to give me hell all day." That was the complete truth, and I wasn't looking forward to being alone with her at any point.

"I understand. I think." He didn't look like he really did and I was grateful for that. "But you could probably escape unscathed. We're not going out today and she can hang off of Tanner all day and whine to him about what a terrible person you are." He grinned that charming smile of his and I brightened at the idea of keeping everyone home today. I had forgotten about that, and I wondered if I would have been a little bit meaner if I knew I wouldn't have to face her wrath alone today.

"I had forgotten about that! I actually am pretty excited for target practice. I've done it for years, it'll be nice not to be the useless one in the group for once." I was pretty determined that I would smoke Miranda and Tanner in any kind of contest. I cared less about beating Zach, though it would be nice to remind my father that I was capable of at least one thing in securing my own protection. Plus it would be good for making Trent feel a little more secure if we ever had to take him out with us again. "And I'm sure you can pick up a bit too!" It would kind of suck to not have that stereotypical opportunity where Zach offered to show me how to do something by putting his arms around me, but I was fairly happy with this alternative.

"I've never fired a gun." He commented, and I wasn't surprised. We weren't a very gun happy country and the only reason I had any amount of expertise at it was because my father was a police officer. And the only reason he had even let me touch one was to hammer in the fact that guns are not toys and I was to treat them with as much respect as I would anything that could kill me if used incorrectly.

"It's nothing special, I'm sure you'll pick it up and outrank me in no time." I patted his hand awkwardly and attempted to stand. The sitting had made me lazy, and standing wasn't easy at first. I used the back of the chair to navigate my way to the sink and cleaned up a bit while he absently stroked Mads head. There was still no sign of Tanner, and I could only assume that Miranda had wormed her way back into bed to fend off her oncoming headaches and general misery. "But until everyone is awake and has chased their sleepy eyes away, I think I'm gonna make use of those awesome presents you brought back for me." When I got all jittery like this there was no way to calm myself down unless I put pencil to paper. Nothing erased the feeling of having five cups of coffee faster than drawing. At least for me.

Wanting to give him some space if he needed it, I settled myself into the office. Cole had obviously slept here last night, the rough looking couch was strewn with a blanket and pillow whose origins were unknown. I curled up onto the comfy looking leather armchair and began sketching. It took a while before I knew what I was doing, but the lines began to solidify in the form of a face and before I knew what I was doing I had sketched out Zach's eyes. Suddenly embarrassed, I stopped for a moment and sat back to look at my handiwork.

"He must never see this." I whispered to myself, covertly checking around the room to make sure no one was stalking me from the shadows. "Never." I wasn't usually so driven by my hormones when I drew but this week seemed to be the exception to nearly every rule in the book. I only managed to get a rough outline sketched out before I heard the tell-tale sounds of footsteps down the hallway and hurriedly slammed it to another page where I had anxiously drawn out the lion.

"Alice?" My name was a question and my drawing walked into the room, come to life in the form of Zach clutching Trent's hand. "Your dad wants you. Miranda and Tanner are up and I think he wants to start." He looked down at the sketchbook in my hands and I wondered if he was glad that I was using it, or curious about what I had been working on for who knew how much time.

I unfurled my legs and leapt off of the seat, wobbling a bit as the blood rushed back down to my legs. Glad that Cole hadn't been around to see that little display and make some assumption that I wasn't ready to go back out there, I followed them back into the kitchen where Cole had laid out the guns.

It took forever but we went through them all one by one with him outlining the different parts and uses and ranges and ammo and all of the boring things associated with shooting. I tuned in and out of the conversation, having heard much of it before and only tuned back in when he brought out the two air guns. "I've managed to find a few targets, but we're also going to use some good old fashioned cans as well." He motioned to the row of empty cans along the kitchen counter, and I could only assume that he had scavenged them as no one had had pop in the last week. "Either will work, I'm saving the targets for when you guys have gotten a little bit better, today we're just going to work on actually hitting what we're aiming at."

We all trooped out outside. The cold air nipped at our heels and I was bitterly aware of how fast the seasons were going to change. Especially with less sunlight, I didn't know how long the solar panels would hold out to support our use. We'd probably have to make actual use of the fireplace sooner or later.

Cole set up our targets and we got to work, taking turns with the two air rifles. Tanner was surprisingly better than I had pegged him for, but

Miranda was just as terrible as I had hoped. I still surpassed the both of them combined, to the point that Cole began skipping my turn. Even Trent had a go, I had argued my way to that one. I figured if ever anything happened to us we had to teach him to be able to survive on his own, especially since he had done such a terrible job of it the first time around. I knew that was a little harsh, he had been dealing with the grief of his mothers death as a very young child completely alone, but the world was a scary place now.

We were down to our last box of BB's when Cole whipped out the flimsy paper targets and set them up. Tanner and I went head to head on ours, both firing in unison until we had emptied the ten BB's that we had been given. I was as I had expected, fairly close to the bull's-eye on all shots and actually hitting it once or twice. Tanner wasn't exactly happy with that, and was visibly upset once we had finished and were comparing. He crumpled his target and tossed it in the pile of decimated cans we had punctured. Miranda and Zach were up next, and he shot with a fair amount of accuracy for someone who hadn't really held a gun before. I knew it would be different with an actual gun, the rifles had barely any recoil and they would be harder to deal with on a moving target. But this was the best practice we could get in for now.

Trent was last to go and was nervous with all of the attention. Tanner, frustrated with his lack of skills, skulked off with Miranda following meekly behind. I wondered if she was torn between siding with him and staying behind to torment Zach and make my life a living hell. That calmed Trent down a little bit, and he stopped shaking like a fragile leaf clinging to its branch. Cole and I coached him through it, while Zach adjusted the target for his height.

"Remember to just keep breathing little man." I adjusted his stance a bit so that he would be a bit more comfortable and take the shock of firing a bit better. "Just pretend you're a sailor and that target over there is a terrible scary pirate who wants to steal your ship. Breathe out and pull the trigger." I let go of his hand and the weight of the gun made it unexpectedly droop a little bit. He furrowed his brow and brought it back up, the muzzle wavering slightly as he pointed at the target.

I could see him concentrating. He narrowed his eyes and tried to breath out, though it came out more as a shaky little gasp. I could see him muttering the word pirate under his breath and he unexpectedly pulled the trigger, the muzzle flying up in his surprise. We all whooped and cheered and he laughed, doing a little victory dance when he saw that he had actually managed to hit the target. Sure, he was pretty far off of the centre circle, but he had gotten it within the outer ring and that was good enough for a first try. "Way to go Trent! Try it again!"

We helped him reload, the gun was hard to pump, and set him up in front of the target again. He took shot after shot, blowing through his BB's quickly and standing there awkwardly while we checked his score. "Well son, you managed to outscore Miranda." Cole handed him his target so Trent could check it over, his eyes beaming with pride. Trent was surprised with his results and giggled to himself, passing it to me to show me his progress. I congratulated him and showed it to Zach, deciding to hang it on the fridge so everyone could see how well he had done.

With our ammo spent we wandered back inside, greeting Mads' anxious whining at the sliding door. Cole carefully stored the rifles in the office, reminding Trent that he was not to touch them without an adult supervising and saying it was okay. We had been outside for several hours and it was past noon, so I went ahead with fixing the four of us some lunch. The men sat around the table discussing various pointers while Trent listened in, occasionally chirping in with his tiny voice to ask a question or add something to the conversation.

It lulled off as we ate, exhausting all of the gun topics we could think of. Cole seemed to be pretty cheery, and I knew he was happy to be back in his relative area of expertise. He missed his job, had always been pretty happy with it and it had been one of his main purposes in life. I tried to bring the conversation back around to something we could all talk about, but I was more happy to just sit in comfortable silence while we all munched away.

As we ate the heavens opened up and began drenching the earth. "I guess it was a good idea for you guys to not be out there today." Waterproof clothing or umbrellas hadn't been something that anyone had thought of, especially with the hot dry summer we had just gone through. It had been a while since we saw the rain. "Though I guess this is good for the plants. It's gonna make me so sleepy though." I hoped that Trent would go down for a nap at some point, he had tossed and turned several hours after I had gone to bed, his body racked with nightmares of which I didn't know the origins. I didn't want to ask him, just in case he didn't remember or if talking about it would make him upset.

Zach and I settled in the living room while my dad cleaned up. Trent looked longingly at the DVD player until I gave him the go ahead and he happily skipped off to find his movie. I grabbed the deck of cards, offering them to Zach to shuffle and deal. We played quietly for a while until Miranda barged in and insisting on being dealt in. We switched to poker, our friendly atmosphere turning intense because of her. She played like a shark, and for a beginner like me I just didn't understand what was going on until someone told me I had lost all of my chips. I sat back and let the two of them battle it out, Miranda getting out whatever frustrations she had dealt with on the firing range. Zach eventually succumbed to her playing and declined her offer to re-deal, neither of us particularly wanting to sit through her quiet trash talking.

Her appeal was wearing thin and I think she knew she was losing her edge, especially on Zach. As far as I was concerned she was nothing but an ice queen with a mildly attractive face. I no longer expected Zach to be swayed by that stereotypically pretty girl, especially since she had taken what I could only assume was such a huge misstep over the past two days. He still seemed uncomfortable with her, and made a point of not letting me leave the room even when I grew bored. I was itching to score the cards and start building a castle to pass the time, but she was still anxiously shuffling and reshuffling them in her delicate hands. If her intentions were to outlast me in the living room she had another thing coming, and as much as I wanted to get up and get my sketchbook I wasn't willing to work on it in here with Zach in such close proximity, or leave him to her manicured talons.

We reached a stalemate and she resorted to glaring at me whenever he wasn't looking. I was okay with this, it was much easier to deal with than whatever verbal taunting I was sure she had perfected over the years. Miranda seemed like the kind of girl who had been pretty enough to be automatically popular in high school, and was fairly used to getting whatever she wanted with very little effort on her part. She presented herself intelligently enough, and must be if she was working towards getting her PhD, but it was the kind of cold, calculating intelligence you expected out of a bird of prey or a lion.

She switched tactics, starting a soft conversation with Zach that I could barely hear, peppering it with attractive laughter and not so subtle flirtations. At this point I was unsure if she was still trying to attract him or was just doing it to piss me off, and I tried not to let it get to me. He seemed receptive enough, but I hoped that he was remembering our conversation last night just as clearly as I was. I'd have to get him alone eventually and find out what he actually thought... Yeah, like I was that bold. I could barely deal with my own hormonal feelings that catapulted my heart out of my chest every time he so much as looked at me.

I sighed and stood, putting weight on my now asleep leg. I was making sure to test it out every few hours, to see if it was getting any stronger. I couldn't handle another day, especially not another one alone with Miranda. I didn't doubt that she would murder me in cold blood and bury me somewhere outside with the vegetables. Miranda took this as an opportunity and tried to drag Zach's attention back to her, so I settled on my stomach beside Trent to watch whatever inane cartoon he was watching. I tried to lose myself in the plot and drown out her annoying voice, barely noticing it when she eventually shut up and attempted to draw Zach to her with a heavy amount of eyelash batting.

Cole wasn't likely to let me out any time soon, even if it was to go with Zach to visit his father's grave. I briefly toyed with the idea of sneaking out, though I didn't think there was any way I could get down the stairs quietly enough to be undetected. However, I didn't want to make him wait for something as important as this meeting. He probably still had a lot to sort out; we hadn't really lingered over the grave the first time around.

I could feel Trent nodding off beside me, so I quietly shut down the movie and motioned for Zach to pick him up to put in bed. He hefted the child, looking grateful for an escape and padded up the stairs. I took this as my own hint to leave, wandering into the office to retrieve my sketchbook. I was happy to see it still laying on the bookshelf, away from prying eyes. Cole was in there, quietly reading some large leather bound book and I didn't want to intrude, only nodding a greeting when he looked up at me upon entering. He was used to my interruptions and quietly got back to his book while I tip toed around so as not to disturb. I was unsure of where to go now. The bedroom was pretty off limits as I didn't want to chance waking up Trent. Miranda was possibly still down in the living room darkening the atmosphere considerably, and I wasn't sure if Zach was going to escape to his own room now that he was free of us all. The kitchen wasn't safe, anyone could wander in at any moment and I didn't want to constantly have to shield what I was working on.

I shifted my weight uncomfortably from foot to foot in the foyer, unsure of where to go before I remembered that there was a cozy looking sunroom towards the front of the house. I wouldn't get the best light in there because of the rain, though it was better than my current alternatives. There was nothing really in there, but all I needed was the weird bench thing and

I could work in my lap. I settled in, patting the cushion but Mads ignored me to sleep on the floor. I tsked at her but started into my work, immediately losing focus on the world around me. It went like that for who knew how long, and I was concentrating on getting the way his hair fell across his forehead when he actually wandered in. I mentally swore to myself, clutching the book a little closer to my chest automatically. "Hey." I felt groggy, in the way you feel when you're interrupted from an intense reading session and weren't fully back in the real world yet.

"Hey, sorry." He looked pointedly at the seat beside me and I shifted so he could sit, angling the book away from him so he couldn't even sneak a peek. I hoped it wasn't coming off as rude, but I sure as hell didn't know how to explain away this one. "I didn't mean to break your concentration." He lounged beside me, stretching with his arms over his head. My eyes instantly went to the bare strip of skin exposed right above his jeans and I fiddled self consciously with my pencil, my eyes anywhere but where I wanted them to be.

"Ah it's no worries, I should take a break soon anyways." I closed the book and tossed it onto the end table beside me, stretching the cricks in my neck and rubbing the feeling back into my hand. "Pretty good way to give yourself carpal tunnel." I joked, suddenly nervous. I had been so close to being caught that my stomach was about to throw up butterflies.

"At least you have something to show for it." He gestured towards my book in a way that made my heart leap up into my throat. I was sure I was going to throw up. "Can I see what you've been working on?" This was my worst nightmare come to life, and it was the most prominent piece in there. I hadn't really worked on anything besides a doodle since he gave me the sketchbook and it was on the first page. How the hell was I going to get out of this.

My brain frantically backpedalled for several seconds while I tried to find a way out of this terrible, terrible situation. I came up with nothing, and probably looked pretty stupid while I sat there stunned. "Uh, I… guess?" My voice cracked embarrassingly on the last word, and I shakily passed him the book. "But um… okay this is weird. Please don't be weird about it. But I drew you." My volume dropped considerably on the last word and I hoped he had suddenly become deaf.

To his credit, instead of looking terrified like I had expected he merely looked curious. I appreciated that, and let go of my death grip on the cover so he could flip through the pages. Even though he hadn't immediately flipped out on me I was still anxious, nervously chewing on my bottom lip while he flipped it open and stared intently at my rendering of him. "I don't know why, I just think your face is... interesting." Yeah, fantastic save there Alice. If I had been alone I would have banged my head on the wall a few times, just to have an excuse to be so inept. "Sorry."

He ignored my squeaking, studying what I had sketched out so far before handing it back to me. "It's pretty good, almost like looking in a mirror." That was a dirty lie, I hadn't even drawn in his mouth yet, but I accepted the compliment and the book with as much dignity as I could muster.

"It's not. It's not done." I shrugged, knowing I would probably never complete it now that he had seen it and I was about to die from embarrassment. I tore at the bottom corner of the page, fiddling with the tear in any attempt to focus on anything besides him. I couldn't believe this was happening. I wished vehemently that the lion had just done me in two days ago. That would be so much more pleasant.

"So finish it." He shrugged back at me and leaned comfortably against my shoulder, his legs hanging over the arm of the bench. I was stunned, not moving for a moment until he closed his eyes, obviously unwilling to move. In our current position he had my arm pinned and I couldn't have drawn if I had wanted to, so I slowly slid him down until his head was in my lap and I could draw over his body. I hesitated with my pencil over the paper, sneaking quick glances down at his peaceful face while he relaxed. The artist in me couldn't let this opportunity be passed up, not with my subject sitting so willingly for me. So I resigned myself to finishing it as quickly and painlessly as possibly, like tearing off a Band-Aid.

It was a while before I realized he was alternating between looking up at me and at my page. It was only until I looked down to see how his bottom lip curved in such a way that I managed to catch him looking and our eyes locked, my fingers spontaneously losing their grip on the pencil as I spasmed a little in surprise. I watched it fall in slow motion, desperately hoping it wouldn't continue on its direct path to smack him right in the face. But it did, and I wanted to curl up and die for the second time that day. And all before dinner.

"I'm so sorry." I freaked out a little bit, catching it before it could make a beeline for the space between his head and my hip. He shook in response, and it took a while before I realized that he was laughing at me. He grabbed my hand, letting it rest comfortably on his chest, which was good as I would have continued to let it hang above him like some deformed t-rex claw. I could feel him vibrate as he laughed, and I couldn't help but smile a little through my mortification. This was unreal, this wasn't happening and I didn't know how the hell to deal with it.

Apparently the correct response was to remain frozen in fear, as he calmed down with his laughter and went back to being quiet. I didn't know whether or not to take that as a hint to continue, and it took me a while to act on it. I wanted to make sure that he was not paying any attention at all before I began again, and his breathing evening out seemed as good a sign as any to proceed. I quietly settled back into my work, not even daring to look down at him again. He didn't stir when I pulled my hand up off of him, and a not so tiny part of me missed that little bit of contact. I was becoming way too attached, and I resolved myself to calm down and see things as they were: just two friends hanging out together and being comfortable with one another.

I lost myself once more in what I was doing, only dropping back into reality whenever he would move. It was a peaceful way to pass the time, and I felt myself growing less and less anxious as the time went by. That wasn't to say that I wasn't still nervous, I had been pretty close to throwing up because of those damn butterflies at one point. I guess I just had a better handle on my feelings, if only for a moment.

I was tapping the back of the pencil against my lips when he moved again, stretching one arm behind me to encircle my waist. I responded by tilting the picture so that he could see my progress and he sat up abruptly, nearly pitching me off of the bench with his fidgeting. He peered closely at it, and I handed it over to him so he could get a better look. That adorable half smile was back, and I was sure that the back of my neck and cheeks were a thousand degrees of red by now. "Quit being so nervous." He stopped his scrutiny momentarily to look up at me, putting his hand up to stop me from whacking myself in the face with the back of my pencil. "This is cool you're cool everything is cool."

I heaved a quiet sigh of relief and leaned back a bit, tossing my pencil onto the end table. It was as done as I could get it for now, and I really couldn't work properly with my brain malfunctioning every time he moved. "You sit pretty still for someone who's being drawn." It was true, he wasn't as fidgety as others I'd had to deal with. "You should volunteer to model for an actual class, see what people with talent can do with your face." Having these quiet times together, as much as they gave me undeniable amounts of stress and overthinking, made me happy in this rather bleak world.

"Like, one of those drop your drawers and strike a pose classes? I don't think I could stomach that. You're not the only one easily embarrassed." I hadn't thought about that, and could feel the slow burn of a blush rising on my cheeks which he zeroed in on immediately. "Please don't tell me you're thinking about me naked." I turned and looked at him with what I could only assume was a terrified glance, and he shot me one of those smiles again. "You are. You totally are." He groaned, and it was a nice change of pace for him to be the one embarrassed now.

"I mean, I am now that you've suggested it." It was mostly guesswork, I had barely even seen him with a shirt off. "I'm staying above the belt for your sake." Thank god there were imaginary lines even my mind refused to cross. He seemed relieved by my statement, and we both unexpectedly burst into laughter.

"Man. I'll take that as a compliment I guess." I let him know that he should and we fell silent, the atmosphere thickening slightly and he took advantage of it. Before I knew it he had closed the gap between us again, and his face was hovering inches in front of my own. "Alice?" My name in his mouth was a question, and I had no idea what the answer was supposed to be. The hairs on the back of my neck were standing up and my skin felt electrified. All of a sudden I was terribly conscious of my hands and had no idea what to do with them.

He sighed and rested his forehead gently against mine, and the closeness was overwhelming. He smelled like saddle soap and boy, were his eyes always that peculiar shade of green? "Thanks for everything. I know that things have been rough and I don't really think I could have gotten through it without you." In the back of my mind I knew I should stammer out some form of 'no problem, I really didn't do anything' but I couldn't form thoughts or words with my tongue. Not when he was this close.

"Cole wants you two in the kitchen." The voice made us jump and turn simultaneously to the door where Tanner lounged with a smug look on his face. Zach patted my thigh and jumped up, apparently not perturbed in the least by what had just happened. I however was still reeling with emotions and confusion even as I gathered up my things and stood. I went to follow him out the door but Tanner tapped me on the shoulder. "Alice, a word?" As much as I didn't want to give him the time of day I waved Zach on ahead, staying behind and shifting from foot to foot. I felt like I was about to explode and nothing had even happened.

"I know this isn't much coming from me, but I would be careful if I was you." He turned to give a pointed look at Zach's retreating back, his voice little more than a whisper. "Miranda hasn't had the nicest things to say about him, and I would hate to see him play you two like fiddles." I wasn't exactly surprised, obviously Miranda wasn't happy with the way things were playing out for her but that wasn't really a problem with me. He was right, it wasn't much coming from him.

"While I appreciate your concern," I didn't, "I've known Zachary for a long time now. He saved my life from something much worse than death. And Miranda hasn't exactly been the picture of welcoming feminism towards me either." I had no patience for whatever else he could say and it was all I could do to remain polite. He had no response, simply shrugging off my statement as if he had been expecting it. For some reason it infuriated me, but I bit my tongue and stalked out of the room. What the hell was he insinuating? And what kind of ridiculous stories was Miranda concocting in that drug addled brain of hers. Zach had barely given her the time of day now that he had hopefully realized her true colours. I would have to sit him down and actually talk to him about it. Tonight.

Still fuming, I found my father sitting at the kitchen table poring over a city map with Trent. Zach and Miranda were already seated as well, and he looked up when I entered. I shook my head, I would talk to him later, and took the seat beside him. "So we've come up with a plan for tomorrow." Cole spoke while Trent beamed at me. I suspected that Cole had included him in the decision making process. That was a good idea, it would make him feel included enough to understand what was going on. "Millvern Station is pretty close here. If they're strategically placing people in the stations there's no reason why some of them couldn't be there. We'll see if we have any better luck there, and just comb through them one by one until we figure out what's going on."

It seemed like a good enough plan. The city population couldn't possibly be held in one subway station, and if we couldn't get anywhere close to mom and Katie at least we could figure out how to a little bit better. I wondered if I was to be put on babysitting duty again, and I looked up from Trent's hand drawn map to ask. Tanner had engaged my father in a discussion and Miranda was wasting no time in making the rest of us exceedingly uncomfortable. She reached across the table to doodle a few locations on Trent's map, much to his delight, but at the same time I felt her leg brush mine before settling on her actual target.

"Oh hell no." My words were little more than an unheard hiss as I saw Zach sit straight up out of the corner of my eye and grab at my wrist under the table. I knew precisely what she was up to, she had looked up for a split second to glare in my direction. For the first time in my life I wished that I was wearing heels, the better to crush her stocking clad feet under. Zach pushed his chair back a little under the pretence of stretching, but I knew it was just so that he would be out of Miranda's reach.

I wanted to launch myself across the table and throw down the old fashioned way. I'd never gotten into a fight, never even been hit, but there were just lines you did not cross and she was now bordering on what we would consider sexual harassment if there was any form of civilization left to play by the rules. Sensing my mood, Mads scootched under the table and unintentionally blocked Miranda's searching foot with her large furry body. I was never more grateful for the dog than I was right at that moment. She was currently keeping me out of more trouble than she knew was even possible.

Their conversation ended, Tanner pushed himself back from the table and waited for Miranda to get up. Her icy gaze bored into my skull but I didn't even give her the time of day or bother looking up. I knew that if I did it would come to blows.

"Uh, sir? If I could ask you something?" I was broken from my angry reverie by Zach's voice and I turned to look at him. Cole nodded and Zach paused for a moment, collecting his thoughts and his words. "Well I don't know if Alice mentioned it, but on the first day I found her she helped me bury my father." Cole looked surprise and shot me a look, I hadn't really said anything to him. There hadn't been an opportunity to do it. "It was such a quick thing though, and I was too stunned to pay my respects. I'd like to go back, now if possible since the rain has stopped. It's not far from here, I would definitely be back in a few hours. Shorter still if I can take the motorcycle that's in the garage." There was a motorcycle in the garage? Why the hell were we still walking places?

Cole considered Zach's words for a moment. "I'm sorry to hear about your father. Alice hadn't mentioned it, though there was never really the time to do so." He cast a glance at Trent, so quiet that we had nearly forgotten that he was there. "I am a little worried about you going out there by yourself though. Even with Madigan, it's ridiculous to send you out there unarmed against whatever you could find. I could go with you, but both of us are not going to fit on that motorcycle."

"Oh well, I was going to go with him anyways." I finally spoke up, ignoring the instant no I could see forming on my fathers lips. "Hear me out. You're the only one with better aim than me. Zach's good but I'm better, and I managed to not get myself eaten last time. And my leg," I could see him about to argue that point and I raised a hand to stop him, "is fine. It's a little stiff, but if we take the motorcycle I won't even have to worry about walking far. It's your call to give me a gun, but it's mine to go. I'm an adult, dad, and we've all got to do our fair share. Besides, I'd like to pay my respects too." My voice dropped a bit on the last part, I didn't exactly want to use Zach's dead father has leverage for my freedom.

I had probably overstepped a boundary with insisting that I would be going regardless, though I had given him an option on the gun. It might be a bit unfair, but so was him still treating me like a child. He sure looked mad, and I could see him clawing with the unfortunate dilemma I had gifted him with. If he wanted me safe he would have to give me a gun. But if he gave me a gun he was admitting I was right. It was a tricky situation and I felt a bit guilty about it.

"I could lock you in your room." He pointed out, though we both knew he wouldn't. As much as my father loved me he also trusted me. And I was a pretty good shot.

"You could, and I could also try to escape through a window." I shrugged, leaning against my chair nonchalantly. "I swear at the first sign of danger we'll turn around and come back. Zach isn't going to let anything happen to me, and I'm going to bring him back in one piece." Or I would die trying, but better not to let that one leave the confines of my brain. "I'm not going to leave you to look after your grandson all on your own." I reached over to ruffle Trent's hair, trying to give him a reassuring smile. He looked utterly panicked that both of us would be going out there. Cole didn't seem convinced, but he knew better to fight me on this and gave up with the same exasperated look that he had had when I had tried to pierce my own ears at age eight.

He was worried though, and rightfully so. I bent down to kiss his forehead and he whispered a time limit into my ear. "You get three hours. If you aren't back by then I'm coming out to get you. If it gets dark before you get back I am coming out to get you. If I so much as get a bad feeling I am coming out to get you." There was no reasoning with him and I accepted his conditions and the small handgun he handed over. His gun from when he still had a job. All the more incentive to bring it back in one piece.

He gave Zach one as well and gave him a stern talking to about bringing me back home. I lounged in the foyer, assuaging Trent's fears while I waited. "You'll have Mads to protect you. This is just something that we have to do." He tearfully nodded, and I gave him a hug. "Be good and I have a surprise for you when we get home." There was still that bar of chocolate I had stashed in our room. He brightened a little bit when I told him that and let go of me. "Be good for my dad. I'll hear about it if you're not!" I gave him a little pat on the back and nudged Mads away from the door. There was no way she was coming with.

Zach lead us to the garage. "Do you even know how to drive a motorcycle?" I didn't even have a license, and to be honest the idea of riding on a beast like this was a little terrifying. "Cause I can barely ride a bike."

"Yeah, I had one before all of this. Was pretty good with the ladies." He laughed, though it sounded hollow and I knew he had committed himself to the task at hand. "And I wouldn't have even let you come if I wasn't. Your dad has basically threatened my life if you come back with so much as a hair out of place." I was half embarrassed but had expected something like this much sooner. I hadn't dated much previously, and whatever weird relationship Zach and I had at the moment was the closest I was going to get in a while. I knew Cole had been saving up his scariest shotgun and cop face for that interview and couldn't deny him taking whatever opportunity he had left.

Zach rolled the beast out of the garage, tossing me a glossy red helmet he had found on a workbench. The motorcycle was nice enough I guess, I really knew nothing about vehicles, but it scared me with its size. And it was going to be fast. I buckled my helmet onto my head and hesitantly got onto the back when he gestured me over. "You have to hold on tight, and try not to throw your body around too much. I have to keep us balanced and you're light, but not light enough not to do some serious damage." I nodded against his back, not trusting words. I was glad to have something to hold onto, even if it was just my arms wrapped around his warm body.

The motorcycle shuddered to life with a roar and we lurched forward, rolling down the steep driveway until we got to the gate. He had coasted for my benefit, letting me get used to how the beast moved and turned and leaned with every move he made. I was just hoping I wouldn't kill us both.

The trip was uneventful. My terror kept me still and the landscape passed in a blur. He didn't go too fast, but fast enough for me to feel it and we made decent enough time. There were no signs of any predators as we got closer to the city's center but I was prepared for them now. Nothing would sneak up on us without me knowing about it, and the cool metal of the gun pressed in my hand would be comforting if nothing else. I could do this, I had practiced it a million times and already taken down my first unorthodox kill.

After a certain point we had to stop and walk the rest of the way just due to the amount of debris that still littered the streets, as well as my newness to the sport of motorcycling. There was no way I could handle such tight weaving without being pitched from my fragile seat pretty quickly. Now that the loudness of the motorcycle had died down we actually had an opportunity for conversation but I let him be, not sure if he was lost in his thoughts and if I would be an unwelcome intruder on them.

I suspected that he had wanted me here more for the company than any need to protect himself or belief in my abilities to do so. I was also probably the least intrusive person who could have accompanied him on this trip, and Cole would not have let him leave solo under any circumstances.

We reached our little marked off gravesite and he slowed, probably not fully prepared to face his father's burial place again. I slipped my hand into his, hoping to be even a little bit reassuring, and gave it a small squeeze. He squeezed back, dropping my hand and stepping forward alone. I let him go, eyes darting back and forth between watching him kneel at the grave and constantly scanning our surroundings. Without Mads as an early warning system we were pretty much on our own, and this was the least appropriate time for something to get the jump on us.

I sat on a half broken bench, awkwardly perching in such a way I could jump up quickly. I could see his shoulders droop, and knew from the snatches of whispered conversation that I could hear that he was saying whatever he needed to his father. I tried not to eavesdrop, concentrating on the watch Cole had wrapped around my wrist. I wanted to make sure that he didn't make good on his threat to come looking for us.

It seemed like eons before Zach finished up, though at no point did I want to be rude and tell him to wrap it up. He said one final, whispered goodbye and crossed over to where I was. He all but threw his body onto the bench with a disgruntled thump, sitting with his head in his hands and his body curled in on itself. I wasn't sure if he was crying, and I hesitated for a minute before beginning to rub his back in the way my mother always had mine whenever I was upset. We sat there for a long while like that, and it wasn't until I was beginning to feel anxious about the time that he sat up.

"We should probably get back huh?" His eyes weren't red but they were dark and brooding. I nodded, standing and stretching out the kinks that had accumulated while I waited for him to finish up. I had made my own quiet peace with the man I had never met while I waited, vowing to him that I would make sure Zach was alright. I turned to him to ask how he was, but was surprised when he took a quick step towards me and drew me into his arms.

I hugged him back, my head nestling nicely into the crook of his neck. He was warm and nice to hold, something I would have never dreamed of happening weeks ago. Sure, we had hugged before. We had been friends. But it had never been like this, had never lasted longer than a few brief seconds of contact while saying goodbye.

I was glad to be leaving the park and it's images of bodies behind. Some of them had already been picked clean by scavengers, their white bones

174

glistening palely in the sunlight. I wondered how many people that I had known and loved lay in those piles, and it was a heavy heart that we both settled back in on the motorcycle. Our depressing task completed, Zach revved the motorcycle back into gear and we left it all behind us. I was glad that no one else had come. They ran the risk of ruining the peaceful respect we had managed to cultivate while we were there.

The trip back seemed to take much longer, though when we returned the motorcycle back to the garage we were still shy of our three-hour curfew. I sighed and ruffled my hair, not sure if I was quite ready to face the insanity of the house just yet but Zach brushed his fingers gently against mine, intertwining them and holding my hand as we walked up the steps to the door. "Thanks again for coming with me." He ignored my stuttered response and kissed me lightly on the forehead. I thought my knees were going to explode and drop my heavy body to the ground, but I managed to keep the stupid grin off of my face and my body upright.

Mads greeted us at the door, wet nose sliming my hand when I reached out to jostle her ears affectionately. Zach gave my hand a squeeze and dropped it when the footsteps drew nearer to the foyer, and my father appeared to make sure we were alright.

He gave us a look, eyes searching the both of us before turning to me. I just shrugged and he took it as an answer, leaving us be. Trent ran in toting Bob and I knelt down to hug him, afraid that if he leapt into my arms his extra weight would cripple my already stiff leg.

The vibrations of the trip had driven me insane with numbing pain and I was happy to take off my jeans and slip into a form of boxer shorts. I kicked off my shoes and hobbled my way up the stairs, almost making it to my room before Miranda's door flung open and she wobbled uncertainly in the hallway. I intended to avoid and ignore her, moving to just step around her and continue on my way but she shoved me with her uninjured arm.

I hit the wall with a surprising amount of force, and before I knew it she was on me with her knee driven into my wound. I gritted my teeth, resisting the urge to call out and half snarled at her. "What the fuck is your problem?" Normally I wouldn't have tried to start a fight, especially with both of us one limb down, but she had pissed me off to no end the past few days. Ever since I met her she had bothered me, if I was gonna be true.

"You." Her nose wrinkled in disgust and her knee drove harder into my leg. I could feel my eyes watering, though I wouldn't give her the satisfaction of

176

seeing me cry. "You need to back off. Step off. He's mine. They're mine. They're all mine." The glint in her eyes was mad and I flinched when she raised her hand, assuming she was going to hit me. Instead she grabbed a handful of my hair, yanking it so that my eyes burned and head angled sharply. "Understand?"

Both of my hands went to hers in an attempt to get her to let go, and as soon as my skin grazed her wrist she did. Giving her knee one final twist and causing me to finally utter a small squeal, she only stepped away from me when we both heard the dull padding of someone quickly moving up the stairs. It was Zach, and I feared he would send her into a frenzy if she didn't manage to compose herself. "Alice I heard a-" He froze once we came into view, gaze bouncing between the two of us. "Noise. Is everything alright up here?" He turned to me and noticed how little weight I was putting on my injured leg.

"Poor thing twisted something on the stairs, that motorcycle must have been too hard on her wound." Miranda turned and cooed at me, looking everything like the patron angel of my health. I despised her and the little act she was putting on for Zach now.

"Like hell I did." I snapped, knowing that if I shut up she would continue her bullying and torment. I wasn't putting up with that. "Somebody got jealous and attacked me." I could feel the blood seeping into the fabric of my jeans, she had torn the wound back open. I swore and touched it lightly, drawing Zach's attention to it. His eyes widened and he took a step towards me.

Something in Miranda snapped and she launched herself at me, knocking me down dangerously close to the stairs and straddling me. Her hand scratched its way to my throat, and she screamed obscenities and called me a liar all the while. She had knocked the breath out of me, and I was struggling to breath as she had her entire weight focused into her hand and onto my neck.

It didn't take Zach very long to react, and he had her off of me in a few seconds, holding her uninjured arm behind her back so she couldn't scratch at him while he subdued her. "Cole! Upstairs!" He yelled while I wheezed and sputtered, rolling onto my side to cough onto the carpet. She had stropped struggling, instead leaning into Zach and doing this weird swaying step. Her eyes looked very far away and it frightened me.

I heard and felt Cole running full tilt across the main floor and up the stairs. He wildly looked from Zach restraining Miranda to where I lay pathetically on the floor. "What happened?" He barked at Zach, kneeling beside me and pushing the hair out of my eyes. I was grateful for his presence and let him check me over, my breath finally regaining some amount of composure.

"I came up here cause I heard Alice make a sound, it sounded like she had fallen and I wanted to make sure she was alright." Zach explained, holding Miranda's body away from him as she continued her weird dance, now adding soft humming. "Miranda said that she fell, and then launched herself at Alice. She was trying to choke her, so I pulled her off. And then she started doing this." At the sound of her name Miranda perked up and smiled down at my father and me, almost seeming more like herself.

"Oh dear, did she fall? I told you she wasn't strong enough to be running around on that leg yet." She crooned, and I was grateful that she hadn't been able to fully use both of her hands. Zach let her go but put his body in between her and me, though I doubted she was going to go into another fit and I had more manpower this time. She looked confusedly at him, leaning around him to continue looking at me as if concerned for my wellbeing.

Tanner had been close behind my father and stood unsure at the top of the stairs. "Come here little fish." He took Miranda's hand, leading her into her bedroom. Cole helped me to my feet and I winced. My ribs hurt, the witch had probably bruised them when she tackled me to the ground. Tanner reappeared and closed the door, leaning up against it and holding up his hands. "I was worried about this, it wasn't her fault. It's the medication we have her on, the antibiotics say they can cause hallucinations and mood shifts."

Zach looked about ready to turn on him but Cole was in the way. "She goes off of them immediately, and doesn't go within five feet of Alice without someone being with her. And I'm locking her in tonight, don't want her wandering around the halls until she's fully detoxed of that stuff. We'll find her some new painkillers, I knew that stuff was bad news as soon as you told me she was having night terrors." He looked at me, apologizing for something he had not done.

Tanner accepted the ultimatum with minimal arguing, knowing that what Miranda had done had not been my fault. He kept trying to plead her innocence to my father and I, saying how she wouldn't have done something like that normally and it had been the medication that had made her snap. That would explain the sudden rage and that scary faraway look in her eyes when she zoned out. But I would always keep an eye on her from now on, and she wasn't going to get anywhere close to Zach as far as I was concerned.

She could have Tanner, he seemed fully capable of handling her madness, but I wasn't willing to deal with it on a day-to-day basis.

Tanner turned to go into the room, closing the door behind him. I could hear her questioning voice and I shuddered involuntarily. Cole went downstairs to locate some rope with which to lock her door with tonight, and Zach followed me into the bathroom with the insistence of making sure I was okay. I sent him away for my coveted boxer shorts and he tossed them at me, turning so I could change.

I hissed as I pulled the pants off of my injured leg, the fabric clinging to the gauze and sliding it down a bit. I had soaked through the white fluffy cotton so I slid the shorts on up and sat down on the edge of the bathtub. Trent poked his head in, his little face scrunching up with confusion and eyes opening wide when he caught sight of the blood. He came and sat in front of me, hovering while he watched Zach unravel the gauze and dab at the freshly opened injury with a wet washcloth. Several pieces of gauze had detached from the original bandage and were stuck in my leg like snowflakes in a patch of blood. He used a pair of tweezers to lift them off and finish cleaning me up.

A fresh bandage and more gauze later and I was all wrapped up. I took a few shaky steps on the leg but it didn't seem all that much worse, if only a bit sore, and I was relieved. Already a light bruise was beginning to form and cover the old yellowing one. My legs would never be fully healed it seemed. I huffed and sighed, pulling my hair up from the sweaty back of my neck and sorted it out into a ponytail. I had a carpet burn on my elbow and a shallow scratch on my neck from where one of Miranda's talons had caught me, but other than that I was alive and determined not to be upstairs.

The boys followed me downstairs and watched me furiously begin cooking. Mads yapped at me from outside so I let her in, figuring that Zach had let her out when I initially went to go upstairs. She came in, all wet paws and cold fur bristling in all directions. Returning to my cutting board, I finished what I was doing and threw our last cut of beef into the oven. We were going to have to find some stuff still frozen or locate some animals and start hunting. I didn't think that we could last as vegetarians for long.

Zach hovered in the kitchen, initiating a game of go fish with Trent at the kitchen table in a thinly veiled attempt to stay nearby. I think he felt guilty for not being upstairs with me when she first attacked, and though I knew he wasn't aware of the full reason that Miranda had gone insane when taunted. I assumed that he had pieced together that it was probably about him. I was content to not speak about it, but I knew I was going to have to talk to him tonight.

By the time dinner was ready Tanner was nowhere to be seen and Cole had wandered into the kitchen, intrigued by the food smells. He said that he would bring the two of them some food up in their room so I wouldn't have to deal with them right away, and I gave Trent a pointed look. He got the message and shut up, I didn't want to scare the kid even more.

Zach jumped up when he saw me lift the heavy platter with the roast on it and took it from me. I wanted to keep busy and frowned at the interruption, but didn't expect myself not to drop it anyway. Now that I realized what had happened my hands had become unfathomably shaky and I could barely stir the boiling pot of frozen vegetables. At one point I had to sit on the cold tile floor, and Mads clicked over to lay her head in my lap.

Within moments I was back on my feet as if nothing had happened, though I wrapped my hand around Mads collar to ground myself a bit and calm down. We all tucked into the food, Cole disappearing quietly to bring some of it upstairs for the two of them. Trent ate noisily; perhaps trying to lessen whatever tension he felt and did not understand. He made small talk, even going so far as to stage a dramatic fight scene between his carrots and his peas. Hiding a grin, Cole told him to finish eating so I could give him the surprise I had promised him.

The chocolate! I had nearly forgotten. Trying to get my head in a more normal place I nodded my head in agreement. "Yup, my dad's right. But you've gotta eat all of your vegetables or I'll just feed it to Mads." Right on cue she licked her lips, whining softly under the table for scraps. Trent took the threat to heart and started shovelling peas into his mouth so fast I was worried that he would choke. Though his food play had set him back, he finished with the rest of us and even went so far to show his good behaviour as to collect his plate and cup and deposit them into the sink without being asked.

I laughed and Cole unearthed the chocolate bar that I had left with him, unwrapping it and handing it to Trent who was literally vibrating with excitement. He inhaled a piece then looked each of us over, carefully breaking us each a piece and placing it delicately on our finished plates. We thanked him and ate our treats, watching as he consumed half of the bar and asked if I would hide the rest for a rainy day. I nodded and wrapped it up, standing and hiding it in the back of the fridge. It was cute to watch him ration his chocolate, but also slightly heartbreaking.

Cole and I went with Trent to finish watching his show, I could almost quote the lines to it by now, and Zach slipped quietly upstairs. I just wanted to zone out and forget the long day we had had, but I conditioned myself to not fall asleep against the soft cushions of the couch. At least, not until I had spoken to Zach. When the show was over I bid goodnight to Cole who looked over me with some concern but let me walk Trent up without a word.

He got changed quickly and hopped up into bed, pulling the blankets up to his chin and looking at me expectantly. "What part of the story are we at now?" Zach and I had been trading off story telling duties, and it was currently about a robot who went off on an adventure to find his missing parts. Trent informed me in his sleepy voice that the robot had just constructed his first pet, a dog named Bob (his suggestion of course). "Right. Well, as Bob barked to life the robot felt a joy in his heart he hadn't felt in a long time. He finally had a friend, and the first hour that Bob was alive the two played longer and harder than anyone had ever played before." The story continued through a daring rescue, an escape from a volcano and a rainstorm that threatened to rust Bob before I noticed he was asleep.

I let out a breath I didn't know I was holding and kissed him on the cheek, tucking the blankets in around his body. Steeling myself for what I was about to do, I crossed the darkened room and shut the door behind me, making sure that I hadn't locked Mads in. It was only a few short steps to Zach's room and I stood in front of his door for a few minutes, wondering exactly what I was going to say. I braced myself and knocked softly, poking my head in when he told me to come in.

He was lounging on his bed, a book propped up against his chin. He set it down when I came in and patted the bedspread when I hovered awkwardly near the door. I carefully swung my leg up and onto it, not wanting to make myself bleed for the third time in too short of a timespan. "What's up?" He pulled himself up a bit more so that his body was leaned against the headboard, shifting over slightly so that I could move to sit beside him if I wanted to.

"I wanted to talk about Miranda." I spoke quietly, afraid she would hear me and come crashing through the wall. "About you and Miranda specifically." His eyes darkened and he nodded, not volunteering any information but seeming open to my questions. "What's happened between you two? She talks like she owns you, and I know she's been kind of touchy with you lately though that may have been the meds." I wasn't sure if I wanted the answer, not certain if they had done more than talked in our first few days here.

"Oh Alice." He half laughed and I frowned at him, not understanding what could be so funny. "She's had it in for me since day one but I haven't so much as batted an eyelash in her direction, which probably infuriates her." He stopped laughing, and his smile turned sad. "That's probably why she went off on you, it was maybe my fault." I highly doubted that, I liked to think that I hadn't made my intentions towards Zach completely clear. "Is that what you've been so worried about these past few days?"

So he had noticed my awkwardness, though he thought it was me being worried and not actually me being too stunned to complete basic social interactions. "I wouldn't say worried exactly." Jealous would probably be a better term, I contemplated as I crossed my legs and tucked my knees up under my chin. "Just confused. She was all over you, I wasn't sure if you were encouraging it or were totally unaware." It had seemed in the beginning like he hadn't noticed her quiet flirtations.

"Oh I wasn't unaware. Well, I was at first. But it only took an hour of talking to her to figure her out." He sighed and rubbed the back of his neck, pulling absently at some of the longer hairs on his head. "And once I realized it and she knew I knew I guess she stopped trying to make it a secret. But I never encouraged it." He stopped tugging and looked directly at me. I wanted to shiver but also didn't want to move a single muscle. "I didn't mean for it to get this crazy, I should have told her to back off a while ago. Can't say I didn't dislike the attention, it helps take the sting out."

"Sting out of what?" I couldn't help but tilt my head at him like a confused puppy. He had stopped making sense, and I could barely concentrate as I had spotted a picture of our group of friends on one of our outings to the beach propped up against a lamp on his end table. He noticed my gaze and handed me the roughed up picture. I ran my fingers lightly along the crease, and then over the faces of each person in it. "We look so happy here. I miss them, hope they're alright." I certainly looked happy, beaming up at the camera from my position on a friend's shoulders.

"I'm sure they are." His voice was closer now, and barely more than a whisper. I looked up and he was only inches from me, staring directly into my eyes. Flustered I angled the picture and untucked my legs so that he would see it better and we could share in the memories together. I could almost feel the hot sun beating down on my shoulders.

I looked back down at the picture, seeking out my best friend Amanda with her arm thrown carelessly around her boyfriend's shoulders. "We played Frisbee for hours that day and I-" I paused when I felt his fingers under my chin and he gently lifted my head so that I was looking up at him.

"Take the sting out of not being able to do this as soon as I would have liked. Can I kiss you?" I was sure my eardrums had exploded, my heart was beating so loud in them. It seemed that my body had shut down, but I managed to respond positively to the question. He thankfully understood my nod and moved towards me, his lips landing softly on mine. My eyelids fluttered closed of their own accord and I leaned into him, feeling like every part of my body was simultaneously on fire burning so hot that it was cold.

This had to be a dream. I couldn't possibly be kissing the boy who had made my knees knock together for months. But his hand curling gently around my face told me it was real, as did the quiet shuddering breath I took once we had parted. I knew my face was on fire and I bit at my lip, unsure of what to say or do or even how to make coherent thoughts. "Where did that come from?" There you go Alice, look a gift horse directly in it's mouth.

He shrugged, untangling his hand from my ponytail. "We'll just say it came from a lot of time spent thinking about you, both before and after this chaotic thing." I shut my mouth, stopping it from staying agape like a fish that had dried out. "I hope I didn't put any pressure on you, but I was kind of hoping that you felt kind of the same way." For once he was the one who was nervous and it made a small smile appear on my face, cracking through the surprise.

"I uh, yes." I swallowed, my mouth felt so dry, and mentally kicked myself for sounding like I didn't mean it. "In case you had any reason to wonder why it was your face I drew." I blushed a bit, thinking about how he had stumbled in and spotted it just a few hours earlier. If I had known then what I knew now. "This isn't a trick is it? Some kind of cruel joke?" My anxiety broke through to the surface and I could feel my eyebrows knit together in worry. He just laughed at me and leaned in to kiss me again, a little bit harder this time.

When I had control over my breathing I blinked up at him, convincing myself that if it was a joke I was going to milk it for as long as I possibly could. "I also came in here to ask if I could sleep with you tonight." I fiddled with my ponytail, avoiding his eyes in case I was imposing and he was about to shoot me down. "I mean, I know Cole locked her door but I'm still expecting Miranda to hunt me down in my sleep and I just need one night without nightmares."

I missed his small smirk but let him pull me up a bit higher on the bed. "You can stay in here for as long as you like." He got up to turn off the lights and I could hear him changing in the darkness as I snuggled under the blankets. He got into bed, confidently pulling me against his chest once he had gotten comfortable. I was glad he was taking the lead here, as I still couldn't believe that I was awake and not in some pathetic dream.

I traced patterns on his chest, my fingers catching on the fabric of his t-shirt. I could feel him watching me and for the first time I didn't inwardly panic and shut down because of him. Maybe it was the half dark with the moon peeking sleepily through the drawn curtains, or maybe I was just drunk on feelings but I felt calm and content. He rumbled under my touch, and I moved my mouth towards his.

Day 9

Dawn broke over us and I lay there, watching
Zach while he slept. He looked so peaceful, and I knew
he would be out for a few more hours, that I couldn't
help but quietly watch him. He still had an arm thrown
around me, and as much as I had a rising desire to pee
I also didn't want to move and chance waking him up.
Last night had probably not been a dream, and I had to
be careful not to explode whenever he touched me
from now on.

I stretched my leg, he had the other one tangled
up in his own, and kicked the blankets gently off of it.
From my limited vantage point it didn't look that much
worse, though the bruises around the bandaging
supported the soreness that radiated out of it like heat
out of a coal. I sighed and worked on bending it while I
waited for him to be up. I meant to let him wake up on
his own but my need to pee was growing and I soon
had to wiggle my way out of his grasp.

His eyelids fluttered and he groaned, pulling me
even closer and taking me away from my goal. "Zach."
I whispered, prodding him in the arm. "Let me up." He
groggily looked at me, but enough of my words had
reached his brain and he let go, rubbing his bleary
eyes. Not wanting to miss my opportunity I quickly

hurried out of bed, opening the door a crack and peering both ways before I dashed to the bathroom. My father skulking around in front of the door was the last thing I wanted to see, I already didn't know what to tell him if he asked. He was probably going to kill Zach.

My teeth brushed and face washed, I all but skipped down the hall. A quick check in on Trent, he was still sleeping soundly in a nest of blankets he had wrapped around himself, and I hovered in front of Zach's door again. I could crawl back into bed and the warmth he put off, and it was still early enough to get a few more hours of shut eye, or I could get up for real and make myself look super innocent.

The lull of sleep tugged me back into the room and I carefully climbed back under the covers. I didn't want to disturb him, his breath had slowed again, but he seemed to sense my return and draped an arm over my hip. His breath in my hair tickled the back of my neck, but it was a nice enough sensation. It didn't take long for me to settle back to sleep.

I woke up a little bit later, as Zach had apparently woken up and was tracing circles on my side. He paused when he felt me wake up, and I turned around to face him again. "Mmh." I sighed and rubbed a wrist across my eyes. I felt a bit less fresh than I had when I first woke up but it was good enough for now. "Morning, sleep well?"

He smiled softly at me, tucking a stray piece of hair behind my ear. "Morning." He let go of me and stretched, looking pretty comfortable. "I hope I didn't wake you up." I shook my head, half relieved that I hadn't imagined all of last night and half unsure that I had. I wasn't sure how to move on from now. "I wanted to make sure about last night, that we're okay. I kind of felt like I was pushing you into this." That surprised me, I was so used to my unrequited feelings that I didn't expect him to be saying any of these things and therefore didn't have any kind of snarky, funny comebacks.

"What? No." Suddenly shy, I looked away from him. It probably didn't look good on me. "I've been pining over you for months. If Amanda was here she'd be the first to tell you that." It had been her weeks of teasing that had even forced me to initiate horror movie nights to begin with. "It's actually been really embarrassing, I can barely make adult decisions, I definitely don't have a handle on my own emotions." He laughed at that and I grinned. It was a peaceful atmosphere, the two of us cuddled together in this tiny bed, and I was unwilling to stop it but I knew we should get up. It wouldn't do for Trent to wake up and panic that I wasn't in the room.

Mads jumped up on the bed, nosing at my exposed arm with her cold nose. "Okay little miss, just destroy my happiness." I kicked off the blanket, swinging both legs down onto the floor and stretching. "I'll take you out, I'm up anyways." Being out of the pocket of warmth made me shiver, goose bumps racing along my arms. I scooped up an errant sweater that Zach had left on the back of his chair, wrapping myself up in it. Yawning I left the room, Mads squeezing past me and brushing her fur against my bare legs.

I poked my head in on Trent again but he was still passed out, one slender arm thrown across his eyes to block out the sun that had started to shine through the curtains. It was still early, I mused as I backed out of the room and shut the door. I spun around to wander down the stairs but as soon as I turned I caught a flash of blonde.

Miranda was in the hallway, arms crossed and leaning up against the wall. She looked pleasant enough, but I could still feel the bruises on my ribs from where she had jumped and landed on me. I gave her a terse polite nod, not wanting to set her off again when everyone was sleeping. The ropes Cole had used to tie up the door lay unravelled on the floor, meaning either my father was awake or Tanner had let her out. Neither was particularly good for me.

She maintained her gaze and I slowly eased my way down the stairs, uncomfortable with having my back turned to her. She didn't jump at me again, and I was glad not to tumble headfirst down the hardwood stairs. Mads yapped quietly at me from the base of the stairs, as if hurrying me up, so I focused on her and made it into the kitchen where Tanner and Cole were sitting close, talking amongst themselves quietly.

"Oh, morning." I hadn't expected anyone to be up this early, and I sure didn't want to deal with Tanner's continued apologies and excuses. "I didn't think anyone would be up." I reiterated out loud, sliding the glass door so Mads could bolt outside. I had obviously interrupted something I wasn't meant to hear as they didn't continue talking, Tanner instead getting up to refill his coffee cup.

Cole caught sight of my sweater and the way the baggy fabric hung on my frame. It was pretty obvious that it was not mine. He didn't see anything, but I caught his raised eyebrows and shrugged. "I was cold, it's freezing." Sure, that didn't mean that I had thought of putting on pants but he was pretty used to me wandering around in my pyjama shorts.

Tanner caught the tail end of our interaction, and his previous warning to me filtered through my mind. It had all been the fabricated reality that Miranda had invented under her haze of drugs. Plus, Tanner must have been looking to bother Zach as well, as he wasn't the sole recipient of Miranda's affections anymore. He looked like he was remembering it too, and I wondered if we would have to deal with more craziness today.

"Do you think Trent would be okay with staying home on his own today?" The question surprised me, and I looked to my father for clarification. "We were just talking about Miranda. I don't know if she's okay to watch him, though with you out of the house she shouldn't have any reasons to make us worried. Plus she seems to have gotten the worst of it out of her system, she hasn't had any of the medication since yesterday morning." I frowned, not exactly sure that I trusted her but I was also unwilling to stay behind today. After my jaunt into the outside world yesterday I couldn't let them go out without me, and I had proven that I wasn't about to collapse if I didn't stay in the safety of the house.

"I don't really like the idea of her watching him. What if she takes something out on him to try and get to me?" I sighed and sat down at the table, the cold wood of the chair making me jump when it touched the back of my legs. "And I don't know if he would be comfortable staying on his own. We could talk to him about it when he wakes up, or we could always bring him with us." I didn't really like my last suggestion; I would prefer him here at home safe and sound. I didn't think he would get into any trouble without us, its not like he was going to try leaving the house and venturing out on his own. There was pretty much nothing for him out there except us.

"I don't really think she would do anything to him, and she was fine watching him before." Tanner pointed out while I worried at my lip, looking between the two men. "She's just not that kind of person, she likes him." But that was before she had tried to choke me out upstairs in the hallway, which I made sure to point out to the two of them.

We quieted down when she came wandering downstairs, murmuring hellos to all of us. She didn't make eye contact with me, instead looking down whenever I glanced up at her. Tanner had mentioned that he had told her what had happened the night before and it seemed she felt terrible about it. I was pretty pleased with that outcome, it would stop me from constantly wanting to break her nose. Or it would help alleviate the desire a bit.

Considering the discussion over for now I shoved my chair back and went to brew some tea, looking down when I felt a pair of little arms wrap around my waist. "Hey kiddo." He clung to me like a baby koala so I let him sit on my good foot and swung him around the kitchen while I made him some breakfast. "Take your eucalyptus leaves you little koala." I handed him the bowl and brought my own tea to the table.

Zach came down, freshly dressed and showered and lightly touched the small of my back when he passed by. He settled into the chair next to me, slinging an arm over the back of my chair without thinking. I could feel him playing with the ends of my hair while he accepted the mug of coffee that Cole passed to him.

"Alright first order of business now that we're all gathered. Like we discussed we're going to be heading towards Millvern Station to see what we can figure out." Cole began the meeting now that we had all settled, the only sound being Trent as he shovelled cereal into his mouth, eyes darting along each of us. "If there's nothing there we'll continue along the subway line until we find someone who can give us some answers.

We were all pretty much in agreement with that statement so he continued. "We will also be searching

199

for a new stock of painkillers, preferably some that don't cause hallucinations." He gave a pointed glance at Tanner and Miranda, the latter who wouldn't drag her eyes from the wood grain of the table. "And just picking up miscellaneous items that we need. This isn't strictly an expedition for inventory, though we're not going to turn up our noses if we find anything we can use obviously."

"Now. We have our second order of business." Cole turned to Trent who paused with the spoon halfway to his mouth. "Trent, we need to know what you want to do. You have three options. First, you can stay here with Miranda like you've done the last two days." Trent looked to me, probably to ask if I was going to stay behind again too but I shook my head, moving my eyes back to Cole. "Second, you can stay here by yourself and wait until we get back. Third, you can come with us." I didn't know if I wanted him to stay behind anymore. What if something happened to all of us out there and there was no one to come home to him. And with all of us armed we could probably keep an eye on him pretty easily.

"Could I bring the practice rifle?" He piped up, looking over at the cabinet that Cole had stored all of the target practice items in. It wasn't too heavy, and the BB's packed a fair bit of a punch. He wouldn't be killing

200

anything, but hopefully we wouldn't run into anything that needed killing anyways.

"I'm sure there wouldn't be any problem with that, but it would be your responsibility to carry it." Cole mused, moving to the cabinet to check our stock. "You would have a fair amount of ammo, we still have a package of ball bearings." He looked at me, and I realized that my father was letting me make the final call. I was touched that he had given me the responsibility, and didn't take it likely.

"Trent what we see out there might be kind of scary. You saw my leg, there's things like that out there." His eyes widened but he remained resolute, shaking his head. "And there are bodies. A lot of people died out there." We couldn't have him having an episode and panicking. "You would have to listen to any adult that told you to do something, no matter what."

He paused, taking in all of my ultimatums. "I can be good. And I can pretend that they're all just dead zombies." I didn't exactly understand his rationale but if he was okay with it, it was probably our best bet. I really didn't want to leave him home alone to wonder about our fate when we didn't return for whatever reason.

"All right then, you can come. Now, if someone wants to check on Mads' bandages while I get ready." I stood, collecting a few dishes from the table and cleaned up a little bit, hovering at the counter and turning back to look at everyone. They had broken up into small groups to talk as Madigan intertwined herself between everyone's legs. Nothing could happen to this little family, I wouldn't let it.

Miranda was going to be trouble on this trip. I thought to myself while I quickly showered and dried myself off. The bruises on my ribs were purple and streaked; they would be a constant reminder until they healed. My breathing was still a bit rough, but nobody needed to know that. I didn't want them thinking I needed a caretaker just like Trent. I sighed and pulled a sweater over my head, meeting everyone down in the foyer.

I handed Trent his backpack, helping him slip it over his shoulders and then following that with the air rifle. He had already loaded it under Zach's supervision, carefully loading the ball bearings into the gun. I accepted the pistol that Cole handed me wordlessly, knowing that if I screwed up at all I would have it immediately taken from me. Fully armed and with Mads whining to go we all set off and began the long winding journey to the station.

Trent kept up a constant barrage of questions and statements on the way and I was glad for the distraction. He held tightly to my left hand, making sure he never strayed too far and was always within arms reach. Mads trotted ahead, nose to the ground and constantly following the sounds that only she could hear in the quiet stillness. As we got nearer to the station I felt a tightness grip my heart, and I realized that I was becoming more anxious the closer we got.

I was not alone, Tanner's face was tight as we approached. A group of wolves stalking a zebra down the street forced us to take another path, and we faced the stairs to the station with some uncertainty. Cole took the head and motioned for Trent and I to fall in behind him, and we went down the stairs in single file like a row of ducks marching to their doom. Trent's hand was cool in mine, and he squeezed it as we approached the gate.

Where the gate would normally be all the way down and locked tight if it was closed, it lay halfway up the track as if someone had forced their way in. The tight sense of foreboding returned and I was glad to heard Zach breathing directly behind me. We slipped under the gate and Trent let go of my hand to hold onto my belt, freeing up my manoeuvres in case anything happened. I drew my gun, scanning the darkness and wishing I could hold a flashlight and a gun at the same time. I handed my light to Trent and he grasped the heavy metal, the light clicking on and dancing over a terrifying sight.

I held back a gasp and dropped down to look at Trent, making sure he was looking into my eyes and not beyond me. "Don't look at them. Do not look." He nodded, swallowing visibly and I stood. The bodies were everywhere, splayed into gruesome positions and sticky with blood. Several of them were riddled with bullet holes, and some dead soldiers in black uniforms lay close by. Cole called out a hello that was met by muffled shuffling, and we hoped that everyone in this godforsaken place wasn't dead.

"We're friends. If anyone can hear me come on out." He shouted out into the darkness, his voice muffled by my own pounding heart in my ears. There was more shuffling and I nearly screamed when a figure emerged. He was a soldier, dressed in the same black uniform as the ones on the ground. His gun was drawn, and it moved from person to person until it settled on Cole. Behind the gun he looked terrified, as if we were ghosts who had risen from the bodies that lay amongst him.

"How are you alive?" His voice shook, and I could see a pale face peek out from behind him. It was a woman, and he shooed her farther behind him. I stepped to Cole's side, but Zach angled himself so that he was slightly in front of me. Cole showed the soldier his own gun, slowly moving to put it on the ground in front of him. I did not follow suit, instead letting it drop to my side but still keeping my hand on it. If it came down to a firefight he would be able to cut through the majority of us before anyone else managed to land a hit.

"What do you mean?" Tanner spoke up in surprise, moving to stand on my father's other side. "It was just a few buildings that were taken out by the explosion. If you weren't near the epicenter you were okay." It hadn't just been a 'few' buildings but Tanner was close enough to being correct. This man's alarm was surprising, and I wondered if he had some info that we desperately needed.

"But the gas!" The soldier cried out, pushing the woman even farther behind him. His mention of the gas reminded me of our foray into the mayor's office, and how we had found that chemical compound that nobody had understood. "You should be dead from it, like all of these people."

"But we're not." Cole took a hesitant step forward, watching as the soldier's gun wavered. "Is it just you two? Let's sit down and have a chat, no weapons. None of us wants to start a fight here." He gestured amongst the bullet-riddled bodies and the soldier nodded, lowering his rifle completely. "Excellent, now perhaps we should take this outside? I promise you, whatever gas you're worried about has long since disappeared. We're not the only things out there." My leg twinged with remembrance at just exactly was lurking out there with us.

The soldier looked hesitant but the woman behind him prodded him forward. They waited for us to pass first, following behind us. It itched, having them at my back when they were armed, but we let it slide. Mads kept trying to jerk the leash back so she could smell the newcomers, and I had to hand her off to Zach. She was getting pretty strong.

The bright sunlight was staggering once we exited the dark tunnels. The soldier and his unnamed woman blinked as if they hadn't seen it in weeks and I finally got a good look at them. He was tall and broad shouldered with fair hair. It looked like he would have a nice smile if he didn't carry that worried look around with him. The woman's face was gaunt and pale, a stark contrast to her swollen belly. She was terribly pregnant and I couldn't help but think of the alien whale baby that waited in there. What were they going to do if the world hadn't righted itself by the time she gave birth? And that looked like it could be any day now.

We settled a little ways away from the subway on a light patch of grass. The six of us flopped down easily on it, and the woman went to follow our lead. Her glossy red hair shone in the grass, and she looked up at her companion with a wrinkled nose. "Seriously Adam?" He didn't look like he wanted to sit, instead stand at attention with his rifle in a more relaxed position but at her insistence he sat, looking totally uncomfortable doing so.

I noticed her eyeing Trent and him looking at her in return, that was some hair, and forced Mads to lie down beside me. She was too excited and was liable to jump on them if I unclipped her, she would probably be too rough for a pregnant woman. Once we were all settled she began, introducing herself as Evelyn and her husband Adam. We went through our own names, and then were was an uncomfortable silence where nobody wanted to ask the obvious. Finally Cole stepped in. "What happened in there?"

The pair looked at each other and he shrugged. "We were shepherded down the line and ended up at Millvern. They made us walk along the tunnels, wouldn't let us know what was going on above ground. We felt the earth shake when the explosions went off but we were told that it was nothing and that everything was fine. We spent four days in there, and they had sealed everything off so nobody could come or go. Told us there was a poisonous gas leaching into the atmosphere and it was safer where we were. We all went along with it, even the soldiers didn't really know what was going on." She squeezed Adam's hand and seemed to draw strength to continue from the contact.

"Everyone was getting pretty antsy. They had rationed our food and water but weren't giving us any information. People wanted to know about their loved ones and there was a bit of trouble. They shot down one troublemaker who tried to leave, to pry his way out of the gates and come out here. It was one shot and it scared everyone into obedience." She paused, as if testing her words in her mind before she spoke them. "Then the ventilation went down and it was as if all hell broke loose. People were getting sick, one minute they were fine and the next they were throwing up blood. We tried to isolate them but there was no room, and eventually one of the soldiers snapped. They began shooting everyone, probably in some desperate attempt to stop the contagions, and there was fighting. There were too many soldiers, too many guns. And once they realized what they had done, the atrocities they had committed, they figured that the future was too bleak. They didn't want to die the same painful deaths that the contagious had, and they killed themselves."

I felt nauseous, half wanting to cover Trent's ears and stop him from hearing this terrible tale. "But what about you two?" Cole asked gently, not wanting to pry very much. But we needed this information. "You can't have been the only ones who survived?"

Adam shook his head, speaking up in his clear voice. "We weren't. I managed to shield Evelyn and stop her from getting hit and soon it was just two others and us. A very old man and a very young girl. He had been shot and was bleeding profusely from his stomach. I knew he wouldn't last very long. The girl was his granddaughter, and it was obvious that she had caught the sickness. We watched the blood drain out of his face when she first started vomiting, and he pleaded with us to put the both of them down as they would surely die." He paused and looked down, and we knew what his response had been. There was no one left alive in that tunnel.

"He had no choice." Evelyn patted his hand and looked beseechingly at us as if we thought they were monsters. "We couldn't have saved either of them, and we didn't want them to suffer. That poor poor girl." She rubbed her stomach unconsciously and for the first time I noticed the streaks of blood across her clothes. Had she held the girl while she died? If I was to go, I would want a kind face like Evelyn's looking over me while it happened, and I took some solace from the fact that neither of them were alone. "But you aren't from the tunnels. How did you survive?"

"Genetic mutation is a beautiful thing." Miranda spoke up, surprising us all, and she shrugged. "People are all different. If it were some kind of virus it probably wouldn't have killed everyone just because of the sheer amount of genes that we all have. Some of us are probably immune to strains of the virus." None of us had experienced any odd symptoms, so she could be right. Were we, and Evelyn and Adam, immune to the gas?

Adam nodded, it did make sense. "So now what? We received next to no orders, just to sit tight and keep everyone calm. Obviously we failed at that, and we can't stay here in this cemetery. This is not where our baby will be born." He cast his eyes back at the tunnels and then to Evelyn who looked back at him thoughtfully. "Are there others like you? Have you formed some kind of survivor colony?"

"There are others," I began darkly, remembering that man in the hotel, "but none that you would care to meet." Zach put a hand on my shoulder, giving it a comforting squeeze, and I focused in on it so I wouldn't have to remember everything.

"We've just been trying to survive as best as we can until help arrives." Cole shrugged. "We've commandeered a house nearby. We have beds and food if you'd care to come with. And I'd suggest doing just that. You don't want to wander far with her like that, and there's more than just criminals running loose around here." He gestured at the lone coyote that prowled against the walls of the bank. It wasn't close enough to be a threat and it was small and weak looking. "We figure both the jail and zoo walls have crumbled. Unfortunately we've had sorry encounters with both types of beast."

Evelyn looked worried, following my father's gaze to the coyote. "That's very kind of you. There are some supplies still inside, rations and the like. We should probably take what we can before we leave this godforsaken place." She moved to stand but Adam pushed down on her shoulder lightly. He wasn't going to let her go back into where her nightmares lurked. Cole and Tanner stood, telling Zach and I to keep watch while they scavenged what they could with Adam, and the three men disappeared into the darkness.

Evelyn turned to me, looking at the gun resting on my thigh. "Your father?" She gestured into the tunnel and I nodded. "You look a bit like him, but you must favour your mother." I nodded again because it was true. Katie looked more like dad, and I was the spitting image of my mom.

I let Mads off of the leash, knowing she would have to get close to Evelyn sooner or later. To her credit she was gentle enough, not even standing up at first when I unclipped her. I watched as Evelyn called her over, holding out a hand to be sniffed before petting along the length of Mads' back. "And I'm assuming your dog as well. Madigan, she's very pretty."

"And useful, she's been with me since everything went to hell." If it wasn't for her I might still be at home, or I might not have been so lucky in getting to where I was now. My path probably would have been completely different without her. "Not quite the world for a puppy to grow up in, or a kid." Trent seemed peaceful enough, working quickly to make a chain out of the dandelions that were letting go of their little cloud seeds.

Miranda remained quiet through the whole thing, ignoring us when Zach, Evelyn and I spoke about our lives before the explosions. I wondered if she would see Evelyn as a potential threat, though it was clear both from their mannerisms and from the matching rings that her and Adam were married. I didn't know if that would help or hinder things, as Miranda could potentially snap again and set her sights on Adam this time. He was fairly good looking and I wouldn't put it past her at this point.

The men returned, their bags laden with whatever they had found inside the tunnel. Adam was still quiet, though I could see that he was piping up with the others every now and then. I wondered if they had talked while they had scouted amongst the bodies, or if they had maintained a respectful silence. Adam seemed like the strong, silent type. He must be strong, to be able to live through whatever had happened in those tunnels. I would put money on Evelyn being the main reason he was still alive. There was no way he would have left her, not in this state.

It was decided that we would return home. The couple was exhausted both mentally and physically, and I needed to have a talk with Trent about what we saw. He was quiet, hadn't let go of that air rifle since we had left the house, and I was worried about what had gone on in there. There had been quite a few children's bodies, I didn't want him to have nightmares like I did. I didn't think they made sleeping pills for children.

On the way back I spoke with Evelyn more. Her and Adam were from the capital of the province, but they moved around a lot. Her family was in Scotland, that would explain the mane of fiery red curls and how pale she was, and they had been unable to learn about the rest of the world while they were underground. They had also not been eating all that much, the rations had been slim and even with Adam giving her half of his she was still thin and tired looking. I told her about the house, about the greenhouse and the gas stove so that we could actually cook and she perked up.

The walk back was slower, we had adjusted our pace for Evelyn and Trent who was tiring quickly. Mads took turns weaving between the two of them and me, not quite sure who she should keep her eye on. Miranda and Tanner kept mostly to themselves, and I could sense a recurring theme there. Maybe they would run off together and solve all of my problems. Or at least most of them.

We were nearly home when the wolf pack showed up. There were three of them, and Mads' hackles went up immediately while they regarded us coolly. Our sheer numbers seemed to dissuade them from attacking us directly, though I figured they were smart enough to try and thin out the herd. I held Trent's hand as we passed them, moving him in between Zach and myself. My limp was unnoticeable enough by now, and there was no way they were getting near me without some interference from Mads anyways so they let us pass. Evelyn stared at them, mouth agape from behind Adam's back. "Told you things out here had gotten weird." I shrugged, pistol at the ready just in case. Again I was uneasy with the creatures at my back, but with Tanner and Miranda bringing up the rear we were pretty well protected.

If Adam and Evelyn were surprised by our temporary home they didn't show it. We got past the gate, Cole checking it to make sure it was still secure once locked, and I ushered Evelyn up the steps. I wanted to get her inside and fed, and she tolerated my mothering with a small smile. I unclipped Mads and led the pair into the kitchen, all but pulling out the chair for Evelyn and sitting her down in it. I reheated some of the soup we had frozen a few days earlier and set the kettle to boil. Zach came into the kitchen to keep me company.

"Where are we gonna put them?" He asked me, sitting on the counter and catching me with his legs every time I was within reach. He kept trying to pull me closer to him and I swatted him away every time just in case Cole decided to wander in, which he eventually did. "Watch it." He grabbed my wrist when I went to swipe at him with the wooden spoon, pulling it to his lips before I could say a word and letting go just as quick. The skin on my arm tingled where he had touched it.

"I was kind of hoping you wouldn't object to Trent and I bunking with you. You can make the chivalrous offer of sleeping on the floor." He raised his eyebrows. "To my dad at least, I don't think he would be okay with it if he knew, even with Trent acting as a buffer." I dropped my voice so Cole wouldn't hear, though he was deep in conversation and I doubted was paying any attention to us at all. "If you don't mind that is." I didn't think he would, but it was better to ask.

"If it means less sneaking around." He shrugged nonchalantly and I gave him another playful swat, though lighter this time. "Your soup's overflowing." He pointed out, ducking under his arms when I brandished the spoon on him again. I turned with a yelp, stirring it furiously so that the volume would fall. I could hear him chuckling behind me but I didn't turn again, making sure that the soup had heated all the way through before ladling it into bowls.

"You could stand to be a touch more hospitable." I teased, handing him the bowls to deliver. He took them with a bow and a flourish, dropping them off at the table with a greatly exaggerated 'sir' and 'mademoiselle'. It made Evelyn laugh, and even stone-faced Adam cracked a small grin before they tucked in. I joined them at the table, clutching my glass of water as I sat down. I felt Zach settle behind me, and we turned to Cole. "They can take my room." I told him, stopping him before he could make any assumptions. "Zach said Trent and I can sleep in his room."

"Oh he did did he?" Cole looked sceptically towards Zach who shrugged and laughed.

"Yeah, she kind of coerced me into sleeping on the floor." Way to take one for the team Zach. I shook my head and scoffed, making a mental note to put Trent in between us. That should teach him a lesson; Trent tended to squirm a lot when he slept.

"Oh we wouldn't want to make any of you relocate just for us." Evelyn's brows knit together in a concerned fashion. "We'll sleep anywhere. I've spent the last three days sleeping on top of an overturned table. I could probably fall asleep on a tile floor at this point." The circles around her eyes were prominent, dark purple and shadowy. I didn't doubt that she could fall asleep anywhere. Adam seemed to be holding off a bit better but I felt that was mostly just a show for Evelyn's sake. I wondered how many nights he had stayed up and kept watch while she slept. No wonder his gun had shook so much when we found him. He must be exhausted.

"Which is why you'll take our bed!" I insisted, crossing my arms so they would know that I wasn't taking no for an answer. "It's really no trouble, Zach's bed is bigger anyways." She looked ready to argue with me anyways but I could see exhaustion taking it's toll and giving me the ultimate win. "For now at least. We can discuss it in a few days when you're feeling more up to it."

That seemed to be agreeable enough for everyone and we settled back into an easy conversation. Dinner passed in the same manner, with the addition of Tanner and Miranda adding a little colour to the conversation. She had perked up a bit and was communicative, though she spoke mostly to Adam. This brought my fears back to the forefront of my mind but I kept quiet, meaning for it to be a late night topic for Zach and I to whisper about. I'm sure he would put my fears at ease and tell me that I was being irrational.

Evelyn excused herself to get ready for bed and I went with her to clear up my old room. I gathered my things and she thanked me again, surveying the room from the doorframe. "It's honestly no trouble at all. It was Zach's idea." I fibbed, smiling at her so she wouldn't figure out that my motives were less than pure.

"Well we really appreciate it." She laid out a few things while she spoke, thoughtfully unfolding a blanket to lay across the foot of the bed. "If you don't mind me asking, there seems to be a bit of bad blood between you and Miranda?" So she had picked up on it that quickly? Clever girl. Not that either of us had ever tried to hide it, my distaste for Miranda was pretty apparent even right off the bat.

"You could say that." I sighed and ruffled the back of my hair, looking behind me to make sure there were no blondes sneaking around unseen. "We had her on some medication for her arm, painkillers or something I don't really know. But they gave her night terrors and made her a bit delusional. She had kind of made us all out to be some kind of harem for her, so I was a direct threat to that. The other day she attacked me, I think she wanted to kill me. So they took her off of the meds." I shrugged, noticing Evelyn's growing look of concern. "It's over now. She's sobered up but my dad still isn't letting her near me without someone else being around. He locked her in her room last night with Tanner, just in case she got it into her head to try and sneak up on me at night. I still don't really trust her, but what can I do?"

I hadn't meant to share so much, I wouldn't want to cause Evelyn any more stress than she was already going through but it seemed almost cruel of me not to warn them. She considered my answer for a long moment, and I shut my mouth for fear of worrying her any more than I already had. "Well, I appreciate you telling me that." I couldn't tell the thoughts that lurked behind her tired eyes and I didn't want to push for whatever information she hadn't already voluntarily said. We fell into a comfortable silence while we each put our things away, and while I worried about her state I was happy to have another non-senile female in the house.

"So they pushed you guys into the tunnels." I said softly, wondering about a few people of my own. "Was that the theme or like, were you guys the only ones they did that to?" I didn't really know how to word it in a way that wouldn't make me cry. I was done being strong for the day and every time I closed my eyes I could see those lifeless bodies clutching at each other in the subway. What if that had happened to my mom. To Katie?

"No, from what Adam knew they were doing it around the city. It's my understanding that they had a few little pockets of places to keep everyone along the lines." She paused, as if gauging her words. "I don't know how everyone else fared. We didn't keep in communication with the other stations after the vents went down. Our electricity went with it and there was no way to call for help." I worried at my lip while she spoke, things weren't sounding so good. "But I'm sure it didn't happen everywhere." She put one of her cool hands on my chin, lifting my face up so I'd look at her and she smiled. "Whoever you are worrying about is probably fine. And you have other things to look after right now. That little boy, Trent. I'd check up on him if I was you." She was more perceptive than I gave her credit for. But she was right. I was going to have to debrief him of what we had seen. Not that he was unused to death, but that was a lot for any of us to handle.

"Yeah I probably should." I pushed myself off of the dresser I had been leaning up against, causing it to wobble on its wooden legs. "I'll leave you to this. Give any of us a holler if you need anything, though I'm betting what you need the most is some sleep right now." From her small smile I could tell that I had hit the nail on the head and I laughed. "Thanks for the info, I'll send Adam up here when Cole's finished pumping him for information. You'd swear you were our hostages instead of our guests."

Downstairs I learned that my assumptions had been correct. Adam and Cole sat alone at the table, words low so that no one else could hear. I knew he would be asking the same kinds of questions that I had, though probably a touch less delicately. I bypassed the kitchen, instead finding Zach and Trent colouring peacefully in the living room. Mads looked up from her spot on the carpet and I settled in beside her, giving her a reassuring pat until she laid her head back down. "And what are you boys doing in here?" The air rifle lay on the ground next to my flashlight, and I rolled the light towards me to check that he had turned it off when I got back.

"Makin' pictures for Adam and Evelyn." Trent didn't even bother looking up from the dragon he was drawing, his nose wrinkled in concentration. "I hope they like purple." He reached for the purple marker and began colouring it in, humming to himself while he worked. Zach pushed his own half finished picture towards me. I had very little idea what he had been trying to achieve and tried not to laugh while I sketched a lion around whatever background this was supposed to be. He seemed to not mind me taking over the project and instead initiated a wrestling session with Mads on the floor, only stopping when Trent shrieked about her claws getting too close to his paper.

"Sorry little man." Zach apologized, ruffling the boy's hair and making him even madder. He must have some practice at being a big brother because he was doing an exceptional job right now. Trent pretended to bite at the hand and I smothered a laugh, finishing my own drawing and sitting up to stretch my sore arms. I didn't know how little kids stayed in uncomfortable positions like that for so long, I was about ready to drop and I hadn't even been here for long.

"I actually wanted to talk to you Trentasaurus." Zach looked at me in surprise but I bet he had the same idea. "About what happened today." I didn't really know what to say, what exactly did an eight year old know about death? And who knew what kind of things his mother had taught him while she was still alive. Should I bother talking about heaven or…?

"Oh I know. Zach talked to me about it while you were with Evelyn." He added the last touch to his drawing and pushed it towards me. I was a fairly decent drawing, kid had some amount of talent for an eight year old, but I was well aware he was trying to distract me.

"And what exactly did the two of you talk about?" I queried, looking between the two boys. Trent seemed unwilling to talk about it anymore and I waited for Zach to admit to something but he just shrugged.

"We talked about the bodies. And about how everybody dies and that what happened in the subway wasn't okay but Adam isn't a bad man." Trent gushed, as if the faster he said the words the less he would actually have to talk about it. I was relieved that I didn't have to be the one to bring up such a gruesome topic with a kid but also surprised that Zach had stepped up to the plate and done it for me. Not that he held any unpleasant feelings towards Trent but he didn't exactly seem the parenting type. "I think he's awesome actually. He's really brave and he protected Evelyn the whole time! I wanna be like him one day and be able to protect people I love." The last bit made me a little teary eyed, and if it affected him the same way he didn't show it. Instead he scooped up his air rifle and looked at me with those puppy dog eyes. "Now can I go practice for a bit?"

I let him go, telling him to find Cole to take him outside for target practice. "Determined little devil isn't he?" I stretched my arms over my head before pulling my knees up to my chest and holding them there. "I'm glad that was so easy, thanks for stepping up to bat

224

and taking care of that. I wasn't exactly looking forward to that little talk." Zach nodded, not really saying much and we sat in a comfortable silence for a bit. Mads had followed Trent outside and I knew there were things we could be doing to help out, but I honestly didn't feel like being productive after the day we had.

"Your dad's worried." Zach spoke up, pulling me over to sit beside him against the couch. "I overheard him talking to Adam. He was asking stuff, but I know what he was really wondering about was your mom." That was to be expected, I would have been surprised if he hadn't tried to sneakily throw in a few questions without explaining why he desperately needed the answers. My father wasn't one for expressing his emotions very often. "You're worried too. I was watching your eyes and I could see you freak out a little bit when they were talking about what happened down there."

He had gotten it right on the first try, I hadn't known that he was watching me that closely, and I bit my lip while I thought. "I just can't help worrying that something like that happened to her too. To Katie. I just keep picturing them and it's…" I brushed angrily at the tears that had formed at the corners of my eyes with the inside of my wrist. "It's terrifying." All too late I realized that Zach's father had probably gone through the same horrible blood filled fate and I felt so much worse. "I'm sorry."

"You don't really have anything to be sorry about little bird." He patted my hand softly, stopping me from another outburst of apologies. "We just have to keep moving. Find out about your mom and your sister, hell find out about everyone we can. Find out what happened and why. If we can even try that, then nobody has anything to be sorry about." I couldn't believe how positive he was being about the whole thing. If our positions had been switched I would be an uncontrollable mess still. But that wasn't Zach. He had always had a pretty level head and a disgusting amount of optimism.

"I could never be as productive as you." I frowned and he laughed, the dark spell breaking for just a moment. "Or as optimistic." His fingers threaded through mine and we spent an hour or so reminiscing about our ridiculous friends and even crazier adventures. We talked until we got hungry, our stomachs winning against our desire to stay put.

Trent had apparently had his fill of target practice, his air rifle lay carefully propped up against the picnic table in the back. I wondered how well he had done, but didn't want to go out and ask. There was no way I was going to interrupt the weird game it seemed like him and Cole were playing. It was some bastardized version of tag but it was cute to see him playing and nice to see my dad relaxing a little bit. It reminded me of when he used to chase Katie and I around the backyard for endless hours and my heart twinged a bit with nostalgia. Mads spotted me leaning up against the glass and barked, but all the tail wagging in the world wouldn't make me go outside right now.

"Do you think we should head back to the station again?" Zach had settled into the table with a sandwich, pushing the plate forward to offer me half. "I mean, I don't really want to go back there and see all that again. But what if we missed something?" I took my half of the sandwich and sat beside him, my mind revisiting the horrific images we had been privy to earlier.

"I don't really think that's good for anyone. They probably cleared the place out when we left." I chewed thoughtfully for a moment, absently looking out through the sliding glass doors. "No, it's better to keep moving. Who knows if there are other people out there like Adam and Evelyn, people stuck or trapped or who don't know that it's okay outside." Was it okay though? My mind skittered on the bloodied faces of the people we had seen in the tunnel. Who was to say that we would find anyone else out there with the same kind of apparent immunities that we had. What if we were just at a different stage then they had been, or if it took longer for our symptoms to progress. More 'what if' scenarios swirled around my head and I shook it as if to clear them out.

"I guess we'll just have to wait and see what Cole says." Zach leaned back in his chair, arms crossed loosely over his head. He peered out to the backyard, just as lost in thought as I had been. Weren't we a picture perfect pair. Both lost in silence about things that were yet to come.

Adam had disappeared upstairs while Travis and Miranda were nowhere to be found, lending a quiet peaceful air to the house. The dark part of my mind chirped that such calm couldn't last for long, that something bad was bound to happen. I forced it out, watching as a few of the leaves fell from the trees in the backyard. It would start getting cold soon. Even with our fireplaces it would be pretty chilly in here, and we'd still have to supply them with wood. I could feel a frown forming on my face and I pushed it aside to the list of things that we would all have to talk about sooner or later.

Hours passed in this way, none of us doing anything spectacularly productive. Trent came in at one point, followed by his entourage of Mads and Cole. He immediately zoomed in on the DVD player and popped in the disc for yet another viewing of the same tired old cartoons. I was starting to learn the entire script to it, we would have to find him something new the next time we were scouting around.

Dinner was a quiet affair. Evelyn came downstairs all bleary eyed and tousled hair. Miranda was more withdrawn than usual, barely meeting anyone's eyes. This hardly bothered me, I preferred her when she was quiet and not making a nuisance of herself, but I did make a mental note to keep an eye on her. Though quiet was good, too quiet could be pretty sneaky. Adam was as silent as a grave, but I was beginning to expect this from him. In direct contrast to the emotive Evelyn, Adam was more the strong, stoic and silent type. It was a nice change of pace to not have to fill the uncomfortable silence with meaningless words when you were with him.

"We'll be moving on tomorrow, thoughts?" Cole broke the amiable chatter with a question and everyone save Trent looked up at him. Truth be told I was glad to be moving on from that massacre back there, and I was sure that Adam and Evelyn didn't want to return to their nightmare. I could see their eyes meeting across the table and I wanted to give her a reassuring pat. I wouldn't want to subject them to that either.

"Moving forward is probably in our best interests." Tanner broke the silence, Miranda nodding her ascent. "We cleared out everything we could from the last station. No sense in going back there." His obvious alignment with Miranda aside, Tanner was shaping up to be a fairly reasonable member of the group. I secretly hoped that Adam would step up to take his place at my dad's side and I doubted that he would disappoint me there. They were two peas from the same pod, it just made sense for them to confer with one another.

Cole turned to Zach and I, surprising both of us but me most. Was he actually looking at me like an adult capable of making her own decisions? This was new, had I proved myself somehow? "We've gotta keep moving." Suddenly embarrassed with my newfound adulthood, I couldn't really meet anyone's eyes. "Who knows if there's other people out there who don't know it's okay to come outside." If it even was okay to be outside. Who knew if we were all going to grow fins and third eyes at some point? Zach nodded, squeezing my knee under the table lightly. I realized that we were all pretty paired off now, with the obvious exception of Cole and Trent. It made me miss my mom and Katie even more, and I wondered if my dad felt the same. I made a mental note to check in on him more often. It would be pretty easy, I had always had a nasty habit of momming everyone I was even moderately close to.

Last he turned to Adam and Evelyn who up until that point had been silent. "We would probably prefer staying as far from that place as humanly possible." Was I the only one who caught that slight quiver in her voice? The glance that Adam gave her told me that no, I wasn't. "It doesn't make sense to go back." He added, his voice a deep rumble. "There's nothing left there. And unless by some miracle the generator goes back online and we have communications again it's completely useless to us."

I had forgotten about them being able to communicate with the other tunnels. Maybe one of the others would still have that ability? My heart soared with the possibilities. We could check up on people, find out about our loved ones! I glanced over at Trent, unusually quiet through this whole ordeal. He wasn't so shy about throwing his opinions out there and I was surprised that he was still gently pushing his meat around the plate. Chalking it up to a general boredom with the adult conversation I left him alone and added him to my list of people to keep an eye on.

Cole was also giving Trent the eye but he didn't say anything about it. "Alright, since we're all agreed we'll start out fresh tomorrow. There's another station we can reach quickly, I'll be keeping track on the map which ones we've already cleared and we'll work our way out. Depending on how things go I think we can do at least one a day, maybe less as we have to travel further out." It made sense, some of the stations could take up to half a day to get to. I hoped things would be sorted out before we would have to camp away from home.

"As far as whatever arrangements you guys have made previously, I think I'm going to have to sit this out." Evelyn spoke up, rubbing her stomach thoughtfully. "I'm just not as fit as I used to be, and you need someone to watch over this little whippersnapper." She grinned at Trent who smiled back at her, already warming up to the petite redhead. It was a load off my mind, I had been torn between wanting to keep him safe and needing to be out there with everyone else.

"I really appreciate that." I would thank her more later, should have known that she was plotting something like this. "The squirt could use some social interaction that isn't me boring him." Trent laughed, launching into a story about his training lesson with

Cole today. He seemed to be getting to be quite the shot, and there was very little left about the boy we had found cowering underneath his mother's corpse. It was reassuring to see him adjusting so quickly but also a little unsettling. Why should he have to grow up so fast? At eight I was still talking to my stuffed animals, not holding a BB gun and checking for carnivorous predators.

Zach caught my pensive face and gave my leg another gentle squeeze. I knew we had all had to grow up fast lately; even the adults had gotten more serious. Had it really only been a week?

Having cooked the dinner I sat back with Evelyn while everyone else cleaned up around us. "Thank you. Really." Now was the chance to get my quiet words in while everyone was busy and Trent was wrestling with Mads outside. "You don't know how much easier that makes things for me." I leaned close to her, my chin in my hand. Evelyn gave me that warm smile of hers, making me feel so much better. She reminded me so much of my mom it nearly hurt. "You're going to be a really good mom soon, you know?"

It was surprising to see her blush, her skin quickly turning as red as her hair. "Thank you, it's reassuring to hear that. With everything going on I feel like this is the worst timed thing ever. Add that to the usual stresses of your first baby and it's kind of insane." She traced a light pattern on the wood grain of the table, pale fingers moving gracefully over the dark wood. "I'm so unprepared. I keep thinking of all of the things we're going to need. Everything's just happening so soon!"

I cast a glance down at her swollen belly. It was probably going to burst any day now. "I guess we should grab stuff on our next run, just in case." Just in case seemed like a great idea. Didn't these things go premature all of the time? I was pretty sure I had heard my mom griping about how unprepared they were for Katie and how early she had been. I vaguely remembered it myself, my mom standing at the bottom of the stairs, knuckles almost white with how hard she was gripping the banister. Their suitcase hadn't even been packed yet. "What're you going to need though? Towels and stuff?" If the media had taught me anything she needed hot water and towels and a knife or something?

"I really don't know. I was kind of expecting the calm, cool sterilization of a hospital." She grinned sheepishly at me, a dark furrow crossing over her brow. "If you guys can find a book, one of those 'So You're Going to Be A Mom' brochures or whatever, anything would be good. I know I'm supposed to have instincts but..." She trailed off, frowning at the tabletop.

"It'll all be fine." I stretched casually and ruffled the hair at the back of my head. "We've still got time. I'll go scouting with Zach tomorrow." I would never admit how worried I actually was for her. If things didn't get sorted out, we would have to bring this baby into the world with the very limited knowledge that we had. My dad was probably the only one out of all of us who had even seen a live birth, unless Miranda had helped with a dolphin birth or something weird like that. She seemed a bit too cold for that, like she would get jealous of the mother to be or something. "Quit worrying about it, you're just gonna stress yourself out more." I was one to talk; I was essentially the queen of stressing out over stuff I couldn't control.

She nodded and while I knew she wouldn't stop stressing like I had asked maybe she would calm down a bit. And really what more could I expect? In her shoes I would be having full-blown panic attacks in every corner and under every piece of furniture I could fit my bloated whale belly under. "Let's go see what the men are doing, get our minds off of this." I stood, offering my hand to help her out of her chair. This newfound sense of maturity still felt strange to me, but almost natural. Like I was actually becoming the adult that my age suggested I was. Hey, I might not be able to drink legally but at least I could shoot lions in the face! If that wasn't a passage into adulthood I really didn't know what was.

The rest of the group was in the backyard, making the most of the setting sun and enjoying each other's company. It was a peaceful scene, and it ultimately brought me comfort. Even if Miranda was there. Resolving myself not to let her upset me, I settled on the low cut stone wall that separated the patio from the rest of the grassy yard. Zach was throwing sticks for Mads with Trent, and the rest of the adults were playing what I could only assume was a hilarious game of poker. Even Adam was cracking a smile every once in a while that reached up to his light eyes. Evelyn wandered over to them, taking Adam's chair when he jumped up and settling easily into the conversation.

Mads dropped her disgustingly soggy stick into my lap, making me cringe at the texture. I wrinkled my nose at her and tossed it as far as I could. That turned out to be not as far as I would have liked, and Trent made sure to point it out while holding his belly from laughing. "I'd like to see you do any better!" I shot out, and he accepted my challenge. His throw fell shorter than mine, but Zach kicked it to give it the few extra inches it needed to win. "You sir are a saboteur of the greatest extent!" I sighed, a small smile creeping onto my face.

The three of us moved over to the poker game, Trent and I making a tag team. I figured he could only be a lucky charm for me, bolstering my already pathetic card game skills. We seemed to be getting a bit better, only having to peek at the card listing all of the winning hands a few times. The conversation covered a lot of topics, ranging from more adult training exercises that Adam and Cole had had to participate in to the time that an adult seal knocked Miranda clothing and all into the training pool. We were having a good time even as the moon rose and it began to get chilly. Evelyn excused herself, leading Trent by the hand to tuck him into bed.

I watched the pair leave, noting the way she had to hold her back as she walked up the steps. Being pregnant seemed like such a terrible thing right now, but there she was taking it in stride and making the best of it. I made a mental note to grab her something while we were out, I really appreciated everything she was doing for us in the short time since we had met her.

I tuned back into the conversation to hear Zach beginning the tale of the time we had travelled to a nearby city with our group of friends. Tastefully ignoring the fact that I had been incredibly inebriated when I made my discovery, he mentioned how I had disappeared only to return spouting tales of a gated off room holding only lamps. "None of us believed her, but then we followed her down into this basement boiler room that was straight out of a horror movie. We kept imagining that some kind of zombie hordes were going to start charging at us out of the lamp room." He laughed and I blushed, remembering how we had all hyped ourselves up into being terrified. "It was just storage for the building and they had stashed extra floor lamps in there, but man was the whole experience creepy."

Playing off of that, Tanner started talking about the time at a bachelor party they had actually ordered zombie strippers for the unknowing groom to be. He recounted how the man had been all set for his incredibly risqué guests when they burst out of the cake all bloody and missing various chunks of flesh. "He passed out." Tanner laughed, telling us all how they had not let him forget about it for years to come. "Even now if you mention strippers he turns beet red." It was humanizing to see him relate stories to us about his past and I began to soften towards him. He was proving to be less of an ass and more like a person who just shouldn't drink that much. I could get behind that.

It was Cole who suggested that we all wind down and go to bed. "We're going to leave pretty early. I'm going to knock on doors in the morning to get everyone up. We have a lot to gather tomorrow and a subway to clear, so everybody get some rest." We nodded and I stretched my arms over my head, cracking my back. My leg had stiffened somewhat but was otherwise good to go, and I could see no reason for me to be left behind from this scouting party.

Trent was asleep by the time we got upstairs, mouth slightly open and snoring up a storm. I tucked the blankets that he had squirmed out of back around him, brushing the light brown hair out of his face. He was due for a haircut soon, unless he wanted to grow it out into a mullet. Zach left to get dressed in the bathroom, and I waited on the edge of the bed for him to come back, pyjamas spread out across my lap. He patted my head as he walked past, curling a finger around a dark strand and tugging on it lightly. Once again I was glad for his comedic antics and just for his general being around. I didn't know if I would have survived anything if he hadn't been around.

Staving off whatever sappy things I was about to burst out with, I hefted myself to my feet and nudged

Mads out of the way of the door. She huffed and I closed it behind me to stop her from sitting outside of the bathroom and ultimately making me trip over her sleeping body.

Once I was changed and ready for bed I quietly opened the bathroom door, pausing in the hallway when I heard the muffled sounds of someone arguing. Evelyn and Adam's room was closest but a little bit of eavesdropping outside of their door proved it wasn't them. I moved further down the hall and stopped outside of Tanner and Miranda's door. Bingo.

I pressed my ear against the wood, careful to make sure the carpet didn't make a sound under my feet. It was hard to make out what they were saying, they were obviously trying to keep quiet. My excellent spy skills let me pick up a few phrases, and it seemed like she was fighting him about staying tomorrow. Apparently Miranda didn't want to come with us? Fair enough, she probably still felt crappy from the medicine withdrawal. What was weird was that she was fighting Tanner to come with us still, when he clearly wanted to stay behind to keep an eye on her. Even with the two of them at home we would still have a four person group to go out, it was something we had worked with before so I didn't really see there being a problem with it.

Shrugging my shoulders and chalking it up to Miranda being insane I padded back to the bedroom, once again pushing Mads out of the way as I closed the door again. Zach was already on his side of the bed, forcing me to clamber over him like a deranged monkey. My leg wasn't healed up enough for these kinds of shenanigans. "I hope you didn't make me do that just to make fun of me." I jabbed at him, heaving a sigh when Mads followed me up and threw herself across the foot of the bed. She took up most of the space where our feet would be, settling in like a giant white and blonde hard cloud. Her loss, I would be kicking her in the ribs all night.

"I would never do such a thing!" Zach put up his hands in mock protest, laughing and shuffling aside when Mads intruded upon our sleeping arrangements. "Okay I know I agreed to you and the boy but the dog is a bit much." She rolled one eye up at him, clearly knowing that we were talking about her and sighed the loudest most stubborn sigh I had ever heard from any man or beast. "I take it that the lady isn't about to move." She sighed again and closed her eyes, pretending to be asleep so she wouldn't have to get down.

"Fine." He hooked an arm around me, pulling me in closer. "I guess we're just going to have to cuddle together. Don't give me that look, it wasn't my idea." He grinned at me, and I rolled my eyes. Typical boy. "I promise to be nothing other than a complete and perfect gentleman. Scouts honour." He nodded, settling me so that his chin rested lightly on top of my hair.

"If you insist." I breathed into his neck, his light scruff tickling the top of my head. "But if we're going to continue this then I insist that we find you a razor tomorrow. You're starting to resemble a pale hobo." I could feel him rumble as he laughed, agreeing that he would look for some kind of shaving implement tomorrow on our trek.

We chatted for a bit, quiet murmurs designed to keep Trent asleep while we both lulled off. The atmosphere was relaxed, the moon streaming in through the window that he had opened to pre-empt how hot it was going to get in here with four bodies crowding the bed.

I woke up a few hours later judging from the position of the moonlight. I was sweating and Zach was clutching my body, stroking my hair. Disoriented and groggy, I moved to untangle myself from the sheets and sit up a bit. "It's okay, you're okay. Everything is fine, I'm here." When he knew I was awake he loosened his grip, allowing me to move around a bit and orient myself again. "You were twitching and crying out." He whispered to me, lips against my sweaty forehead.

My throat felt raspier than sandpaper and I licked at my lips, my tongue passing over their dry exterior. "I don't remember what happened." That was a lie, I could see clearly the room I had been so afraid of in my mind's eye. It had haunted my dreams for nights now, and I thought vaguely of the pills tucked carefully in the bottom of my bag. Couldn't reach them now without letting him know what I was up to, and there was really no time to take them.

"Go back to sleep. Think of happy things." He moved a hand to my back, picking at the fabric of my t-shirt and fanning my back with it before settling it. With him still muttering to me and rubbing my back I started to close my eyes again and settle in against him, fighting against the terrifying faces that hovered at the edge of my dreams.

Day 10

Trent was up first, poking me in the back and making a general nuisance of himself. "Your dad is knocking." He whispered in that little kid voice, hopping out of bed to open the door. Knowing that I had three and a half seconds to scoot to the other side of the bed, I wasted no time in throwing Zach off of me and rolling over. Sneaky spy skill number two, I managed to look innocent just as Trent opened the door.

"Time to get up. Get ready and meet us in the kitchen." He looked suspicious but only as much as he would normally be with me sleeping in the same bed as a child and a boy my own age. He was handling this surprisingly well. I nodded at him, rubbing the sleep out of my eyes and reaching over to whack Zach awake. He was already halfway there, probably from me roughly manhandling him to escape and making me feel guilty with that tousled hair and tired eyes.

Cole left the doorframe and Trent moved to his backpack, pulling out an outfit that his mother probably would have never let him leave the house in. I let him be, it was probably better to build his independence and really there was nobody around that he would be impressing. Worst-case scenario he would find a pack of hyenas to laugh at him for his fashion choices.

I did the same, rolling up my pyjama pants to check out the damage to my leg. It looked okay today, the bandage was grubby and would need to be changed but the bruises were starting to change colours. I assumed that meant I wouldn't die and tossed a clean pair of underwear at Trent, noticing that he had forgotten to grab a new pair. "We'll get you some more stuff while we're out today. What colour shirts do you want?" I asked him, knowing that he would probably fight me on whatever I brought back regardless. How was I to know that he was too old for bears? Teddy bears seemed like perfectly acceptable clothing choices for an eight year old.

I beat everyone to the bathroom, and was pulling my hair into a tight ponytail when Zach returned from getting ready. I stood up, shepherding Trent down the stairs in front of me. Mads was already in the kitchen, pacing back in forth in front of the back door. Her nails clicking along the tile was irritating to me this early in the morning, and I tossed the door open before grabbing myself a glass of juice. Cole had cut up some fruit for Trent to eat, and Zach was cautiously sipping at a coffee that looked way too strong for human consumption.

"Today is a scouting and recon trip." Cole began when Evelyn had filtered into the room, yawning and dragging a brush through her red hair. "We're obviously going to be on the lookout for supplies, so if you can think of anything before we leave just write it down for us." He mentioned the last part to Evelyn and Trent who was pushing orange slices around his plate with casual disinterest. She nodded and grabbed the pad of paper that sat on the kitchen counter, immediately jotting a few things down. I doubted they would be very hard to find, she didn't seem like a super high maintenance person, even in her severely pregnant state. It wasn't like she was going to ask us to fetch pickles and ice cream to satiate her cravings.

I was extremely anxious to get going, preferring being out in the field and doing something useful to hanging around here like a sloth. The rest of our unofficial meeting passed quickly; someone gathered Mads and her leash from outside and we gathered in the foyer. I could tell that Trent was moping about being left behind. He sat on the stairs, one hand in his palm while the other picked at the dark wood that was chipping on the bottom step. "We'll be back soon you little monster." It wasn't that reassuring but it was all I had. "Plus it'll be nice to hang out with someone besides me. Maybe Evelyn has some cool stuff for you to do." He perked up a little bit, batting those wickedly long eyelashes at me with excited eyes.

"Evie did say that she had a few games to play with me." He admitted, a small smile creeping up onto his previously morose face. The sun was giving him freckles, a small light group smattered across his nose. It struck me as particularly adorable. Soon he would be losing teeth and I would be melting into puddles of cute. I ruffled his hair in response, tucking Evelyn's list into the front pocket of my jeans. "Bring me back something cool okay?"

"Course we will." Zach winked at him, coming up behind me with Mads' leash coiled around his hand. He passed it to me and I tucked it into a pocket. We might as well let her roam, she wasn't going to move far from me at this stage in the game. "We'll bring you back a mammoth tusk or something." I severely hoped that we wouldn't run into any predators looking for blood out there, be it man or beast. Didn't know if I could survive another run in with a lion without losing an entire leg.

Our goodbyes said, I realized that Cole and Tanner were speaking about something, their two dark heads close together while they whispered back and forth. "If you're sure it's for the best." Cole was saying, and I assumed that they were talking about whatever I had eavesdropped on last night. Tanner nodded, his face set and grim. I wondered what was up but really didn't care enough to ask. Miranda looked pale and like she had heard the worst news ever, but considering how she reacted to things I didn't put much stock into it. "We'll be fine with the four of us, especially if we find more people like Evelyn and Adam." I agreed, there was safety in numbers but what was the worst we were going to find out there?

We set off; I walked backwards until we were out of sight of Trent's tiny body waving both of his arms at us from the living room window. It wasn't until we had rounded the gate and he was out of sight that I righted myself. I was glad for Evelyn, I would have felt weird with leaving him alone with Miranda, even if Tanner was there to supervise her.

Our party being so small was kind of unnerving, but I sincerely doubted that we would run into anything more than a wayward pack of wolves. And hopefully they would be too smart to try and take on a group of humans like us. Hopefully. Besides, we were equipped with those boom-sticks and were therefore doubly dangerous. We were definitely a pack to be reckoned with.

We moved quickly, nobody really having much to say as we walked. I had half an eye on Mads, making sure her bandages were holding up under the strain of trekking across the streets. She had seemed to bounce back fairly quick but I still worried over her like a mother hen. I didn't know what I would do without her.

We stopped in and scavenged a few stores first, mostly picking up baby centric items and food. It was such a monotonous task, and I didn't know what would happen when it started to get cold and our food stash began depleting. Was it too much to hope that all of this would be resolved by then? I mean the government had to step in at some point.

A sense of apprehension rose up in my stomach as we drew towards the subway system. Thoughts of bloodied bodies splayed out in terrifying positions played out in my mind and I nearly stopped in my tracks. I didn't know if I could handle another veritable blood bath like the one when we had found our newest members of the family. From the queasy looks of everyone around me, I wasn't sure if anyone else would be able to handle it either.

It was before we hit shouting distance that we noticed the first crumbling's of shattered buildings. The piles of rubble grew larger and larger until we were met with an impassable mound. At first no one had any idea what we were faced with, and I reigned in the leash a bit as Mads tried to pick her way through the glass and cement. It hit us all kind of around the same time. We were looking at what was left of the subway station. Even being above ground hadn't helped these people out.

"This used to be a building." Cole pointed out, gesturing towards the splintered wooden sign that lay in the middle of the street like a forlorn abandoned toy. "Looks like someone didn't make it." I looked past his outstretched hand to the car that lay in the middle of the debris. Whoever the previous occupant had been had driven through it at a high speed, maybe undergoing seizures from the airborne virus. It would probably stop them from being able to control their limbs for a bit.

"Should we... should we uh, check it?" Zach spoke up. He sounded like I felt, there was no way I was going up to investigate whatever puddle of goo used to be a fleshed out breathing human being. And it was blocking the entrance, the glass smashed in and allowing all manner of oxygen to leach into the building. Unless there were more people like us sheltered in there I didn't really see us finding any living beings. "I mean we should right? See if we can move the car and see if anyone in there is still kicking around?" I really, *really* did not want to get any closer to that vehicle. I could almost taste the burnt rubber smell that was floating around us. It stung my nose and made my eyes water, I could already see Mads snuffling along the ground and sneezing.

"We should check." Adam nodded, the strong stoic type. Of course it wouldn't outwardly bother him. He was trained for this sort of thing. Hesitation crept through my bones as I watched him pick his way carefully up the pile of stones, whatever they had previously been was unknown to me. He peeked into the car first and I let out a sigh, knowing it wouldn't make sense for all of us to look. At least he was taking the dirty jobs.

The rest of us followed behind, falling into a slow, careful procession after him. We must have appeared sombre to anyone who cared to look; all downward gazes and silence. Nobody said much, and I made sure to steer clear of the car in a wide circle, unsure if I would be able to handle the sights and smells that probably lingered after death. Adam and Cole walked ahead of us, heads close together as they whispered back and forth between the two of them. I half wondered what they were talking about, but a lot of my brainpower was being put towards paying attention to the precarious rocks that I was forced to pick my way through. I could catch whispers of words, floating back to us on the dusty air, but not enough to put together full sentences.

When we caught up to the pair of men they were already calling into the wreckage. We all stood around the entrance, Mads shuffling restlessly around. Already her fur was streaked with dust and grime, the usual white coat marked with gray. "Anybody?" Cole shouted out again, his voice echoing off of the shattered glass and broken steel beams. We all strained to listen, though I wasn't sure whether or not we hoped that anyone would respond. If they did, would they be sick or not? Was there some way that the disease had progressed to infect those of us who had survived the first wave?

From somewhere in the darkness there came an answering cry, then another. I could hear chattering, at least one woman and a man but it sounded like more than that. Cautiously they emerged from the gloom, two men in front with a tiny woman slightly behind them. The woman seemed misshapen somehow, as if she was a hunchback or something. I guess it would explain why she was trailing behind them like that.

They had weapons, I noticed. The few beams of sunlight caught the harsh gunmetal grey when they finally wandered within viewing distance. Neither man looked particularly comfortable with them, and I drifted my hand cautiously to my belt. If they shot I wouldn't be quick enough to draw on them, but if they were as unpractised as I thought they were it was possible that they would miss. And I might not. Not that I hoped it would come to that.

"You guys didn't get sick either?" The first man approached. He was the bigger of the two, dark brown hair and goatee streaked with silver. Probably older than Cole by a bit, and was definitely taking on the leadership roles here. His forearms and chest were coated in dried blood. It probably wasn't his. His hands shook a bit, but he lowered his gun and held up his empty hands. A rare sign of trust these days. "How many... Is it just you four?" Mads had drawn his attention, straining anxiously at the leash to get a better sniff of these newcomers.

A quick look passed between Adam and Cole, and eventually my father spoke. "We didn't even known about the sickness until yesterday." He shrugged, stepping forward to get a better look at them and extending his hand. "But no, there's us and some more back at home. We had to set up camp a little outside of the city, things are kind of running amok here." As if to emphasize his point there was a guttural scream from somewhere nearby. Apparently some kind of herbivore was getting slaughtered. "Far as we can see, the zoo has emptied itself into the streets. Along with a few other... undesirables." The second man's eyes widened, they were incredibly green, and he quickly looked back at the blond woman. She shifted slightly and nodded, and from her edited stance I could tell that what I had mistakenly assumed was a hump was actually a little girl riding piggyback. An involuntary grin crept up my face before disappearing immediately. I hoped that they had found her in better circumstances than Trent had been in.

"More back home?" For a brief moment the leader sounded hopeful, before clearing his throat and reassuming his stony face. "I'm Steven by the way. This is Ryder and Scarlett. The little tagalong hitching a ride is our lucky Penny." Scarlett nodded, her petite face grim. If these people came home with us I could only imagine the destructive field day that Miranda would have with this woman. Maybe she could get off better than I had. But it sure wasn't doing her any favours that she was pretty.

"Pleasure to make your acquaintance. Is it just you four?" Cole moved as if to look behind them but no others emerged. Their dark faces kind of said it all, and Steven nodded his head. "Alright then. If there's nothing we can clear out of there we should probably get a move on." He looked unsure, I knew the feeling as well. How many people would we be able to support at the rate we were going? Feeding everyone was going to start getting kind of tricky.

"We should head back soon, we're going to need to grab more supplies." I spoke up, watching as everyone's gazes flicked over to me. "I mean um, if that's okay with everyone." Suddenly uncomfortable with the amount of attention I was receiving from the strangers I blushed a little, shifting my weight from foot to foot. I had been comfortable speaking up within our current group, but with the addition of these new people the dynamics would surely shift. I wondered if Steven would replace Adam as my dad's right hand man or if we would have to vote in an entirely new leader.

Thankfully Steven nodded again, agreeing with my suggestion. They looked hungry, the dark shadows under their eyes pretty prominent. Penny seemed to be the only one going unscathed here. While pale, her eyes didn't have the same tired yearning that the adults did. "We'll collect our things. A moment please." They turned and walked back into the darkness. I wasn't itching to see what was in there, probably more destroyed bodies like we had seen while collecting Adam and Evelyn.

They weren't carrying much when they came back. A few backpacks, a couple of guns that they must have pulled off of some dead soldiers. Adam's eyes roved over the weaponry, probably thinking of his fallen brothers and sisters. I bet no amount of military training could really prepare you for the horrors they had described to us and I hoped that the little girl – Penny – hadn't had to witness much of it. Trent had obviously been around his mother when she went through the spasms, convulsing and spewing blood from her mouth. It made me shudder to think of.

"You haven't seen any other people?" Cole questioned the newcomers as we picked our way through the rubble again. Mads had quieted by now, resolving herself to sniff crazily at everyone once we had gotten home. Now we were in travelling mode, everyone keeping their eyes peeled for any carnivore's intent on making us dinner. Cole and Adam had debriefed the adults of the perils of travelling out here, hammering it in that you weren't to do it alone for fear of being easy pickings for a pride of lions.

We did our introductions while we walked, Steven walking in the front with Cole and Adam while Ryder, Penny and Scarlett tagged along with us. Penny had roused herself a bit and was walking instead of hitching a ride. The little girl was very interested in Mads and after a brief hand-sniffing intro they seemed to be the best of friends, Mads even letting Penny hold onto the ruff of white gold fur around her neck. I left her unclipped for now, figuring that with a child in the party she would be pretty unwilling to dart away. She had already proven herself around Trent, I wasn't worried that there would be a major change in character here.

Since Cole hadn't told us otherwise Zach and I made small talk with our new acquaintances. Their story was similar to Evelyn and Adam's, with the addition of a car driving through the front doors to accelerate the disease spreading. They spoke in hushed tones, probably for Penny's sake and not to reopen old wounds. It was understandable, this had all been fairly recent for them and they were probably still reliving their nightmares daily. "We're really glad that you guys came along. Don't know how much longer we would have made it in there. And by now we aren't really up to dealing with whatever is out here, guns or not." There was a sharp barking cry of what I had begun to identify as a hyena and Penny stopped in her tracks, not moving until there was some gentle prodding from Ryder. "There's a pack of them that comes to the doors and makes that sound at night. Gave the little coin some nightmares." He ruffled her hair, scooping her up into his arms so she wouldn't slow us down.

We could see them off in the distance, roving around some buildings. Noses to the ground they didn't seem to notice us but Mads saw them, hackles raising to make herself bigger. "C'mon poofball." I patted her side, keeping her moving and hopefully stopping her from going after them. When all was said and done this dog was going to have some serious complexes.

Keeping child and dog focused on one another seemed to do the trick as they both worried about each other just enough to completely ignore their surroundings. Mads had always been good with kids, even as a puppy. Not that she was much more than that still. She had been gangly when this all went down, an awkward furry adolescent. Now she moved a bit more gracefully, stumbling over things only a quarter of the time now. Even her fur seemed less poofy and ridiculous, contrary to my previous comment. It was still mottled gold, red and white, but she looked almost like an adult. Almost.

I was pretty absent from the conversation, tuning in every once in a while to add my two cents. It wasn't until they started talking about the car running through the glass that I fully joined in the conversation.

"That's when everyone started to... you know." Ryder muttered, casting a furtive glance at Penny. It was clearer now that she was his daughter. She had

258

the same coppery coloured hair and freckles. Though where he was scruffy and big she was lithe and pale. Must have taken after her mother, who was not Scarlett as I had originally assumed. "I had been trying to get a hold of her mom before that. Some of us still had cellphone reception in there. But as soon as that glass started to crack..." He shuddered, clearly remembering the same blood nightmare that Adam had spoken of. And was probably speaking of with Steven. "It didn't happen very long after we started getting shoved in there. Those army guys weren't the nicest." This time he looked not at Penny, but at Scarlett. She avoided his sympathetic gaze, staring down at the ground under the pretence of not stumbling. "But it all started to go downhill pretty fast I guess."

Our only stop was in a shopping center, with half of us splitting off for food and the remainders for baby supplies. I could see Cole warily looking at us when he and Steven took Ryder and Penny, leaving Adam with Scarlett, Zach and I. We wouldn't be far apart, a point I used to assuage his paranoia. Besides, I had Adam. The chances of anything happening while we baby hunted was zero to none. And closer to zero at that.

We split up, the men and Penny moving up a few stores to case the supermarket for anything that hadn't rotted to oblivion yet. I didn't envy them. The smells in there were probably not the nicest, even after smelling a melted human in a car. In direct contrast, the kids store was eerily deserted. Neither patrons nor employees lingered in the aisles, bodies or not. Shopping list in hand, with Adam marvelling over cribs in the next aisle over, Scarlett and I split the task of finding everything. Zach mostly stood lookout – wrestling with Mads in the store window – to narrow our chances of a surprise lion attack again.

Trying to ignore the insanely high prices (who knew babies cost this much!), I roved between the pink and blue aisles and tried to make this a one time only trip. We bundled up a bunch of onesies or whatever they were called. "I found some more um... baby sacks?" I handed them out to Scarlett for inspection, who deemed them small enough for a newborn baby. I was in over my head here, almost wishing that I was braving the rotting meat aisles of the grocery store instead. Fighting off whatever predators were in there leeching off of the decomposing meat almost sounded like a treat in comparison.

Our shopping trip was quiet, until we commandeered an unlocked cart to drag home with us. There was no way our treasures could be fit into our backpacks, and we had gotten a few larger toys and things as well. It rattled and clunked along behind us, echoing its earth shattering noises as we met the others in our predesigned spot. They didn't look any worse for wear, maybe a little tired and green around the gills if Ryder's complexion gave anything away. Not sure if anyone else noticed how his eyes immediately gave Scarlett a once over, in the same way that my father did.

The trip home was quiet and I thanked our lucky stars that everything had gone fairly smoothly., if you ignored our rocking and rolling buggy. It heralded our re-entry into the neighbourhood, and promptly got bogged down with pebbles. Instead of a smooth glide up to the door, where I had envisioned us spreading our gifts to the others, it was a bumpy series of shoves until we reached the front door. Which was slightly ajar...

"We're back!" Cole called out as I cursed Trent for leaving the front door open. It had to have been him playing out here, unless Miranda had mindlessly forgotten to close it. "And we come bearing gifts!" Everyone seemed to be in a much better mood now that shelter was at hand and I could get a warm, home cooked meal into our guest's bellies. With this many people living here for now it was sure to be exponentially less quiet, though I mused that we could set them up in a neighbouring house so no one felt too crowded.

It was incredibly quiet. So quiet, in fact, that the creaking of the front door drew everyone's attention as we all piled through it chatting and laughing. So quiet that at first nobody noticed what lay in front of us, and it took several seconds for anyone to react. Several seconds for Ryder to cover Penny's eyes and hug her tightly to his chest, several seconds for Scarlett to reel back in shock and horror, one hand clasped over her mouth and eyes wide. And several seconds for Adam and I to call out the names of our left behind loved ones.

I could feel the scream tearing at my throat even as my eyes didn't move from the thing in front of us. The wind we had let in through the door jostled it slightly, so that it swayed from side to side in the dancing breeze. Zach's hand grasped at mine, pinning to me in the same way that Ryder was holding Penny. I had such a handle on Mads' leash that the rough fabric was cutting into my palm, even though she was making no moves to get away. It was her whines that broke us all out of our reverie; her crying that moved us all into action.

"What the hell, WHAT THE HELL IS THIS?!" Steven's voice was the first to boom out, and he took a few steps towards Cole that I viewed as threatening. Zach let go of me and stepped between the two larger men, keeping Steven off of my father. I could see how blank his eyes looked, how deeply this was shaking him. "You bring us back to this?!" It seemed that he thought this was all some sick joke, like the image of Tanner swinging back and forth in front of us was some ill gotten prank. Like his purpled face and bound hands were *our* idea.

It clicked within me that moment. I had to find Trent. I didn't care about what was going on right here, right now. I had to find the boy I had left behind. Mads nudged at my hand and I dropped her leash, leaving it to trail behind her body as I moved throughout the house a split second behind Adam. I followed his calling out to his wife, using the brokenness of his voice to keep me stable. "They're fine they're fine they're fine everything is alright." It was a murmured prayer to the both of us as we finished tearing through the ground floor. "They're fine." I whispered to him again, letting him take the lead as we bolted up the stairs.

We stopped dead at the top of the stairs, and I squeezed his hand even as I coughed and gagged through tears. We could see both the top of Tanner's hanged body, as well as the broken banisters that someone who was bleeding heavily had leaned against. And there wasn't a bloody mark on Tanner. "They're fine." My voice came out in a gurgled cry, and I wasn't sure if either of us believed me anymore. But everything hinged on me believing that I wasn't about to walk in on the worst sight I had seen since I found Zach all those days ago. The bile rising in my throat seemed familiar, but I choked it back as we moved systematically and followed the trail of blood.

Whoever it was had dragged themselves, and it was spattered low on the walls as well. A smallish handprint stopped us both dead for a minute as he wordlessly pointed it out to me. Too big to be Trent, thank god, but too small to be Tanner's. That left either Miranda or Evelyn, and the tiny, horrible part of my brain hoped to whoever was listening that it was Miranda's.

The people downstairs had almost caught up with us by the time we reached my old room, their voices loud and confusing and trying to stop us from opening the door. Adam tried the knob once or twice, growing increasingly agitated when we realized it was locked. Mads was whining ferociously, sniffing at the blood and going crazy from the theatrics all around her. I felt that at any moment I would burst from my skin in a panic.

One running jump at the door and it splintered under Adam's shoulder, another and it completely gave way. He nearly fell into the room in his haste, and I followed blindly behind him. He had knocked several pieces of haphazardly stacked furniture out of the way, scattering it across the room. I blocked Mads from entering, pinning her to the doorframe with my leg while our eyes adjusted to the dimness of the room, taking in the solitary figure sitting upright in the bed.

Upright and clutching a baby? "Evie!" Adam breathed out, nearly choking on his cry as he crossed the room in three easy strides. Evelyn looked exhausted, and the bed sheets were soaked in blood. I hovered in the doorway, unsure if I should enter while they were reuniting, but desperately needing to know the answer to my own question. I could hear footsteps behind me, as Cole nudged his way into the room and went to check on Evelyn with Adam. Once sure that both woman and baby were fine, he asked her what I could no longer repeat. "The others?"

She seemed to snap out of her reverie, sitting up and hugging the swaddled infant to her chest. "They. Tanner..." We nodded, and she took a deep breath before continuing. "Alice I'm so sorry. I tried to stop them, and he fought back like a little wildcat. But Trent..." I didn't hear the rest of what she said and their voices turned soupy. My vision went dark for a few seconds and I felt my knees buckle, Mads taking the opportunity to weasel her way out of my grip and return to the main floor. Zach was behind me in an instant, leading me out of the room and sitting me down on the edge of our bed.

I followed dumbly, and the next thing I knew he was sitting at my feet, holding my hands in my lap. Trent was dead, and it was entirely my fault. This was all I knew, and all I could think of. My mind played a brutal reel of our time together, of how happy he had been in direct contrast to when we had pulled him from underneath his mother's corpse. And now he had gone to join her. Dead. Deaddeaddead and all my fault. "Alice, it's okay. We'll get him back."

Wait. What?

"We'll find him and we'll take him back." Did Zach not understand that he was dead? Was he proposing a trip to heaven where we would pull the boy from those pearly gates ourselves? I shook my head. Half in disagreement and half to clear it of the swarm of buzzing that was currently replacing my hearing. "Yes we will. It'll be fine." His words stung, even if he didn't know he was doing it. They were a harsh echo of my mumbled prayer while we were searching for the survivors.

"Stop it Zach. You can't bring back the dead. It isn't fine. It's all my fault." I felt his hands settle on my face and I realized that I had been shaking my head again. All I could feel was a dull throbbing in my temple and a creeping chill in my bones. "It's not fine."

He silenced me, holding my face so that I was forced to look up at him instead of at the floor. I could numbly feel Mads approach, laying her warm head in my lap as well. The closeness was overwhelming. "Alice. Stop. Listen." He paused, making sure that I was focusing on him. "Trent isn't dead. They took him. The people who killed Tanner. They took Miranda and Trent. They tried to take Evelyn but she was in labour and they couldn't move her. That was all the blood." He must have seen the question on my lips. Could he also see the tiny glimmer of hope in my eyes? Trent was alive! The thought sent sparks singing through my veins to my fingertips. Then the sparks turned to rage, and my vision threatened to fade to red.

In a moment I was standing, sending Mads sprawling from my abrupt change in position. I was out the door before Zach could stop me; down the stairs before he could catch up. My march stopped at the kitchen table, where the men had gathered to discuss the situation at hand. I only vaguely registered their faces: how dazed Adam looked, how grim my father's face was, and the distress on Steven's. This made no difference to me, or my mission. I stood tall in the doorway, making sure all eyes were on me so there would be no question.

"We are getting him back."

20865863R00159

Made in the USA
Charleston, SC
30 July 2013